FALLING DARK

TOM LLOYD

Created with Vellum

For Fiona, Ailsa and Euan

Thank you for everything.

1

A level tone lost in the dark. Too much of space flight is like that. Sounds swallowed by the void. But this one doesn't fade into nothing, instead it gradually builds. It's just a distant intrusion at first, the single speck of a star in the night sky. There but unimportant. Then it grows and a part of me responds, that instinctive tilt of the head toward a new-risen moon.

The sound continues and slowly my brain starts to kick into gear. I become aware of a faint glow – a subtle intrusion that together with the noise begins to tease me from the dreamless dark. More sounds filter in: the hum of the ship's systems, the throb of the engines. It's peaceful though, the usual comforting rhythms in a world where discord means danger. Out in the great dark, commotion rips you from sleep like the sun's full force and the last few years have honed my instincts there. To serve on a ship is to know the risks and once you know them, your brain will hit screaming-terror mode at the slightest provocation.

Finally I move, muscles released from their sleep paralysis, and that brings me closer. Some part of me recognises the notification tone. At the back of my mind there's a command to get up but all I do is grunt and roll on my side. The room's still dim-lit. The computer clearly hasn't decided it's daytime for her fleshy pets, as Jamal likes to describe us.

That idle thought pulls me further towards wakefulness. Wasn't I due to wake for the day shift? Or at least, what the computer chose as day. In the deep black the computer can tinker with our rhythms as much as its algorithm fancies. With a small crew we can't maintain a full rota, but induced sleep isn't good for anyone long-term.

Heavy-limbed and awkward, I emerge from my crypt with the usual groans. Flapping at the high lip running around the bed I eventually get a grip on it and pull myself up through the web of safety straps. I rub one hand over my face before blearily focusing on the screen at my bedside. It's just illuminated with a non-urgent notification so my eyes first focus on the image slotted into the side.

'Good morning, my loves,' I whisper to the pair of beaming faces squeezed onto their father's lap. 'Sleep well?'

No reply of course, they're millions of miles away, but that's the life I've chosen. When the morning, or whatever this is, comes where I don't think to say hello to my family first, that's when I've got a different sort of problem in this job.

Today I can imagine their replies easily enough. It's only been a few weeks since I saw them last. The warmth of my husband's embrace is rather more distant, but the gangly limbs of the kids hanging onto my neck? Those memories remain fresh. No chance of forgetting any of that. No chance of our reunion being any less than wonderful despite the news I'll be breaking.

I unclasp the safety straps and sit up properly, clearing a space to stretch like a cat in the sunshine. My cabin has the luxury of some extra room, but not so much I'll get far above my station. A flip-up bed just about big enough for two that hides a recessed couch in the personal side, table, chairs and desk in the captain's half – everything crowded by high lockers.

When starting out in this job, I'd dreamed of taking a family with me to the stars. Just us in a ship not unlike the *Sakakawea*, exploring distant places as I do now. The romance of the job didn't fade much, but actually having a family put the realities into perspective.

Leaving my eldest as a baby was a wrench. I might even have taken him with me that first time if I'd owned the *Sakakawea* by then. By the second however, I was ready to have the parts of my life a bit more separate. They fill all the space around them, Jamal even more so. Each one is as messy and exuberant as the other. Messy doesn't work in space, not unless you're rich. Nor do pre-teen tantrums or marital squabbles about the family finances for that matter.

The accusations of flying off and leaving them for months at a time might have dried up, but Jamal and I in close confines would have generated other problems.

'Play notification,' I say at last, the words muffled by a yawn. The computer does nothing and for a moment I get anxious, wonder if there's actually some new malfunction to add to the list of ailing parts. Fortunately it's just the computer not recognising the command. Just an adaptive AI, nothing clever. I'd need to captain something truly huge for that to even be a possibility.

'Computer, play notice,' I repeat and then it does.

–notification-anomaly detected on long range scan-within custom parameters definition–

'Custom parameters?' I ask, still too sleepy to remember

my own settings. As soon as I speak I remember but the computer replies anyway.

–interesting/unusual/weird–

'Oh. Yeah, that. What have you found then?'

–anomalous signal detected–

That jolts me to my feet and out of the bed. Still clumsy with sleep, I lurch and have to catch myself on the corner of my desk.

'On screen,' I order.

A stream of jagged spikes starts to crawl their way across the wall screen. It means nothing to me but the computer helps, highlighting sections where there's a repeating pattern. That's what I'd set it to search for as we went about our usual business of surveying systems beyond the fringes of human space.

We're best placed to trawl for a signal no human's ever heard before and if we find one… well, it's worth the diversion. Now more so than ever. It means going off-schedule but what's the worst the company can do to me at this point? Luck's been against us for a while now and I know what's waiting for the *Sak* when we get to claimed space. They can hardly strip out their proprietary tech and terminate my contract any more than they're going to already. We're on full burn through sub-space beyond the fringes of human space, returning from a series of failed investigations of potential systems for exploitation/colonisation. These days, the returns are fewer than when the company built its vast wealth, but they're hardly a sentimental bunch. Come through or make way for the next scout. Don't mind the freezing vacuum on your way out.

'Wake Sim,' I order as I start to pull on clothes. 'Are we back-tracking?'

–course is set and engaged-Simphiwe is awake–

I drag open a drawer under my bed and pull on the first clothes I find, followed by shoes. I run my fingers through my coarse hair, reminded that it's got a little long. It's still short so as to not be uncomfortable under a helmet, but has grown enough to stick up weirdly after sleep. I don't like going to work looking unkempt, just like I don't let the ship resemble a junker any more than necessary. It's too easy to let everything slide when you're stuck in a ship for weeks at a time with just three others, but this isn't a normal day.

I check my main screen and slow myself down. We've not started the countdown for re-entry to normal space so I've got time. Adjusting one shoe so it's more comfortable, I think of the previous two occasions the computer has pulled us off-mission because of something that could plausibly be a signal. I'd forgotten the command was still in the system. Probably would have stripped it out if I'd thought of it recently. Any trip but this one and the delay wouldn't have been acceptable, but now it doesn't really matter. Might as well hope for that last, final chance.

I know I'll never stop dreaming, even if I end up unable to pursue it. I'd been hooked long before I explored my first wreck. My earliest childhood memory is the announcement of the Draied Orbitals discovery. From that one news story, half my life's course has been set. Right now it's taking me after some faint piece of static the computer had detected from sub-space and I couldn't be more excited.

Dressed, I tap the door control and head out onto the main corridor that runs in a loop around the cargo hold. It's dim, but brightens as I step out. Almost in the same movement the neighbouring door opens and my first officer appears.

Sim is a stocky woman with a riot of colours in her dreadlocks and a warm, gentle manner. You have to pick your shipmates carefully on a small crew like this. Jamal soon started calling Sim "my wife's wife" because we co-exist like some elderly couple. He was right and wasn't even being snippy about it at first, though I hadn't liked to indulge him by agreeing.

'Signal?' Sim asks, yawning.

'Signal! Maybe today's our lucky day?'

'Yeah, I've heard you tell that one before, Song,' she says with a weary smile. Sim knows the hole I'm in, but she's an optimist at heart with skills that'll get her onto another crew easily enough. She heads off towards the flight deck with me close behind. 'Doesn't ever mean it's worth getting out of bed for,' she calls back over her shoulder.

'You don't think much is,' I counter. 'No wonder all those men get tired of you!'

She snickers. 'They get tired alright, just not of me. "Worn out" might be more accurate.'

'Given the mess in your room, I wouldn't be surprised if I found one buried in all that junk, too weak to dig his way out.'

'Sorry, Mum,' Sim says without a shred of contrition.

Together we pile into the flight deck where screens are already lit up. We slide into our flight-chairs and settle back as the main screen shows streaks of light flashing past. The arrival count-down pings up as we sit, informing us we're soon to drop out of sub-space. Eighty seconds. My stomach bubbles with excitement even as my chest is tight with stress. For a few seconds I'm a little girl again, staring up at the big screen back home as the first pictures of Draied are shown – beamed back from a scout ship not too different to the one I'm in right now.

Sim taps a side-panel and starts some old rock music

playing in the background. Her fingers tap a drawer below it, but she doesn't pull it open.

'No?' I query.

She just grins. 'As much as I love watching sub-space stream by with a buzz in my head, you never know. Maybe this really isn't another wild goose chase. I can wait five minutes to find out. And when the signal turns out to be nothing, I'll light a joint and put my feet up as we get back on course. There may be some light mocking too, but nothing you've not heard before.'

I manage to smile and nod. You spend enough time out in space, you're either entirely ambivalent about the view or it never stops being a delight. I often have it on in the background in my room while I read, the warped streaks of light in sub-space as comforting and hypnotic as the flames of a fire. Sim prefers to watch it with a mild psychoactive and the sound of guitars thrumming through her body, especially that moment when the light stretches and shudders as we snap back to normal space.

"Nothing better," she declared once when I asked. I've never really agreed, but then I've never been so serious about music.

I settle back, check on the other two members of the crew but the ship reports they're both still asleep. On a long skip after an arduous mission that's normal, but this diversion might change that.

'Repeating signal,' Sim comments as she inspects the data more closely. 'Unknown pattern, computer can't make much of it. Nothing on the wreck and salvage database. This system's just a dot on the chart though – we're way out past explored space. Registered by LongScan as of little interest, just one of thousands without a planet we'd want to investigate.'

'Human signal?'

'Nothing to suggest it. Possibly something military and scrambled. Pirates wouldn't bother fishing like this though. You'd only catch folk like us or someone with big ass guns. Either way there are better livings to make. Probably some freak natural emission.'

I ignore her even as I dampen down the excitement in my gut. Alien life isn't remotely likely, but ancient tech on the other hand... there's lots out there spread very thin across the vastness of the great dark. That's why I've got the computer ready to alert me over weird shit, just in case. Most of it's dead and drifting; junk that's degraded over thousands of years with barely an emergency beacon to squawk at the neighbouring black for anything that's searching. Even those are of interest to a wreck-diver like me under normal circumstances. There doesn't have to be a fortune waiting out there, just the excitement of investigating – of being the first human to discover it.

–commencing re-entry sequence– the ship chimes in as I watch the countdown.

The engine's hum changes pitch noticeably. Next the swirls and streaks on the screen slow and distort crazily as the sub-space drive disengages. Then with a jolt and a wrench – we're out.

A burst of brightness greets us. It's a shock despite the ship dimming the screen to make it look like a dying sun. We've dropped out into a system of multiple planets, two right ahead of us either in synchronous orbit or we happened to appear on alignment day. Data starts to fill a side panel. The sun's relatively small, well below galactic average. The planets too – the larger probably gaseous from the green swirls I can see and small for the type. The other, sunward and harder to make out, is a fraction of the size of its larger fellow.

And something else as well. Something that could never be a moon. Even as we spot it the computer identifies the shape and enhances that section. A long thin shape, dark and gilt-edged in the light of the sun, it glows against the background of the gas planet's shadowed side. Sim gives a sort of strangled wail. I just gape, refusing to believe my eyes at first. Even when I do accept the sight, my brain fails to process it. Beside me Sim whoops with joy and slaps a button.

'Jad, Kall – wake up you beautiful idiots! We're rich!'

2

Elusive against the darkness of the planet, edged with fire where the sun's light touches it. No natural shape, not with such distinct lines and curves, but at the same time like nothing built by humans I've ever seen. This isn't a secret military ship or research base. Any system with the capability of building this would hardly be able to hide how far advanced beyond the rest of us they were.

We wait for the others in silence, hardly daring to breathe. Jadeen is first to appear, half-dressed and half-asleep. She's a tiny thing, slim and nimble with purple-tinted hair that hangs fashionably over one eye and makes me feel old. I hear the swish of the flight deck door and the patter of her feet.

'What the... is that...?'

Her words tail off. She doesn't even make it to her flight chair, just lurches the last few steps and holds onto mine to keep her upright. It's a little while before Kallum joins us. The big man grew up in a strict household with five sisters and doesn't leave his room unless he's well presented. It doesn't stop him swearing before he's taken two steps inside the flight deck. The song playing in the background changes and slows. Mournful guitar riffs begin to ring out. The moment stretches through the lonely notes.

'Godsdamn, look at the size of it,' Jad gasps eventually. 'That's huge!'

'Computer – estimate size of signal source.'

–estimating-source is approximately ten by two by one metres–

I exchange a look with Sim.

'Honestly, I was expecting it to be bigger,' she says with an incredulous smile. 'Um – computer, reconfirm.'

–confirmed-ten metres in length-two point four metres in width-one metre in depth–

'Is the ship looking at the same thing as us?' Sim whispers out the side of her mouth, as though trying not to offend the non-sentient machine. 'Or have I smoked so much glitter over the years I've started to hallucinate?'

'Let's start with door number one,' I reply. 'Otherwise I'm having the same problem. Computer – identify source of signal.'

–transmitter array one point eight kilometres from this position–

'So too small for us to see,' I conclude. 'That's a relief! For a moment I thought we were going to be stuck out here with a malfunctioning AI.'

'Computer,' Kall says. 'Estimate length of the larger craft.'

There's a long pause while it pings the ship with its sensors.

–estimate eighteen point four kilometres–

'Howling void, that's huge!'

'Strap in,' I order. 'We're going to take a look.'

While Jad and Kall slip into their seats, Sim plucks a tiny pill from the drawer where she keeps her joints.

'Is that even necessary?' I ask, nodding toward the pill. 'Did the sight of the gigantic alien spaceship not wake you up enough?'

'Blew my mind at the same time,' she counters, 'and I'm always foggy after induced sleep. Unless you put the coffee on before you came out, I'm gonna need something to help process the mountain of data we're about to get from...'

She flaps her hands towards the screen, running out of words.

We lapse back into silence as I activate manual control and start slowly towards the beacon. While I'm doing that Sim starts with the usual scan on the system, searching for signals, movement or hazards.

'Song,' she says after a few minutes. 'This system looks empty to me. No one but us, no other signals or artificial satellites.'

'It's not native?'

'Not from initial sweep. This size of ship, the planets would have clear traces even if they're subterranean-based.' She points at the screen. 'That giant appears to be the only one large enough for anything like that and no recognisable life would survive there. It does have a surface, pretty big actually, but wrapped up in a whole lot of nasty atmosphere and pressure.'

I bring up a marker and direct her to the smaller sunward planet, dark with a crescent edge of golden light. 'Is that colour? Blue maybe, or just sensor error?'

Sim squints as the computer enhances as best it can, but we're just too far to tell. At full enhancement the computer's extrapolating so it could just be effectively guessing at the colours.

'Minerals? Metals?'

'Got to be worth a drone, no?'

Sim gives a curt nod. She looks almost irritated I'm not focused on the prize, but our employers will have noticed where we are. One fun detail of being a freelancer loaded with company tech, they keep tabs on where you go. We've had instructions to return directly so if we linger, they'll soon investigate.

'Jad, prep a drone for survey. Now can we finally take a proper look at the gigantic mystery that called us here?'

I almost delay just to mess with her, but I'm also eager to move in.

'Kall, keep your eyes peeled. I don't want any surprises, okay?'

'Sure, boss.'

I take the ship closer. The *Sakakawea* isn't fancy or new, but she still handles well for a non-combat craft. As we near the wreck the full scale of what we've found hits us. I hear Sim gasp like she's just taken a punch to the gut and can only nod in agreement. It's enormous. Just mind-blowingly big. The largest human ship I ever heard of was four kilometres and even that was mostly empty space for hauling asteroids. This thing is solid all the way, long and bulbous on the right-side as we're looking at it, streaked with reflected light from the sun. Even when we reach the beacon we can't see much detail of the main ship.

A hundred yards from the beacon I stop and have the computer magnify the image. It's pretty much what I expect – a miracle the thing's still going. A transmitter array coupled to some sort of power unit and a solar collector. Pretty battered now we're close enough for a good look, but not any deliberate damage. Just the wear and tear of centuries out in the cold. And as if we had any doubts, the components and construction look entirely alien.

'It ain't pretty,' Kall comments from his console, bent forward over the screen while one hand hovers at the sensor readouts. 'Thrown together in a hurry I'd guess given the exposed sections.'

'Is it so far away to be clear of the planet's magnetic field?'

'Not looking like it,' he says with a frown. 'Low levels from what I see, nothing to interfere with a signal.'

'Has it drifted from the main ship then? Why even launch it?'

As I speak I start the engines again, sweeping past the relay. It's not going to tell us much, not unless we can decipher the signal and if it's alien in origin, that will take a long time. We might as well inspect the real prize for clues.

'It's not a relay booster from what I can tell,' Kall says as we surge forward. 'It's the source of the signal itself.'

He's still puzzling over the data while the rest of us are looking eagerly at the main ship.

'So the ship's comms got fried?' I hazard. 'Why bother shunting this so far away then? Debris? Meteoroids?'

'Very low levels of debris or large material according to the initial system scan,' Sim says. 'The wreck's been there a long time. The chances of it remaining intact without shields is tiny if there's much around here. May just be a super high orbit so it can be maintained easily.'

'Still, it seems weird, no?' I say. 'To have the signal a long way out, entirely different orbit if that data's correct.'

'It's weird, yeah,' Sim agrees. 'Does that explain it?'

She points at the wreck in the distance, marking an overlay of the main screen. Her marker highlights the line of long furrows in the huge ship's hull, hovers over great ragged holes that have been punched in the side.

'Look. Adds to the theory this transmitter was chucked together in a rush.'

I slow the engine burn and keep us steady as I take in what she's saying. The huge ship is hard to make out, but the screen flickers and compensates. Sim zooms in and I hiss at the sight. There's so much to see I barely know what to start with. Projections like the spines of a fish mark the middle section, great rounded lumps stud the fore – given the scale those could be biodomes or detachable ships for all I know, maybe even gigantic weapon housings.

The size just keeps hitting me, a shock with every new thing glimpsed. The closer we get, the more detail we can make out and the more it becomes real. Not just a shape in the distance. Not just a dream of something incredible.

'It's definitely not human-built,' I say uselessly. 'It looks like it's been designed by an artist not an engineer. No secret military project would look like that.'

'Something military happened here,' Sim reminds me.

'We don't know what tore the guts out of this ship. Asteroid impact?'

'One that size?' Kall replies. 'No chance. Far too neat. Something that big hits any ship, it's catastrophic. Just a tangle of alloy left for weirdos like Song to crawl through on their days off.'

As he speaks Kall highlights more holes, a neat line of three. 'Tech being stripped out or ejected maybe, subordinate sections serving as life-craft. Altogether, this is battle damage. They lost the fight and abandoned it.'

Even with the computer compensating on the screen, the ship is dark. It reminds me of an insect; something segmented and bulbous found on the new worlds. Whatever it's made of, it's a gunmetal grey picked out with silver and golden bands. What the metals are I can't even guess at, but I've never seen any ship with gold on.

Decorative on a scale that size or some new alloy?

Either way the excitement jumps into my throat. Gold isn't much used these days. The value disappeared soon after TanGrey drives were invented and humanity discovered vast deposits, but language hasn't moved on as fast. The word still holds some magical allure and here is a vast alien craft that shines with a golden glow.

The value of this wreck is incalculable even without any viable tech or information on board. If it's actually gold and used decoratively, this ship is going to be the most gorgeous sight once I get inside it. Either way, I am definitely going inside.

I honestly can't even tell which I'm hoping for. Buy-a-planet-rich has never been a goal of mine. Paying the bills has always been enough and the salvage claim on this will do more than square me with the company. The dreamer in me still hopes of finding something extraordinary and unique, but I've still asked myself the question. What could I do with incredible wealth? My home planet's got its share of problems after all.

I take the *Sakakawea* in closer, bringing her underneath as we're currently angled. We round the bulky rear section that made me first think of an insect. A broad abdomen with long smooth stretches like a beetle's folded wings. There's a great dome-shape extrusion at the fore end of that, then it drops sharply to meet a cylindrical section marked with impact holes and what I guess are shuttle bays. Some of those are open, but it's black inside and the computer can't compensate as we make our sweep.

It gets wider but flatter at the thorax. Those lion-fish

spines I now see protrude from the flanks as well. At a guess the biggest is a kilometre long. Surely too big for a comms array, but I can't imagine what else it could be.

The "head" rises like the slopes of a hill, smooth on the front with three deep channels running down the back slope. The very front narrows to a blunt point, its surface marked with complex geometric shapes.

I'm assuming that's the front anyway. We've not got to the very back end yet. It could be there's nothing resembling engines there and I've got it all wrong. This is totally unknown tech after all, but I've read all I can about other space wrecks. Most follow a basic configuration, but it's all determined by engine tech.

We're all quiet on this initial sweep. Sim indicates some details to me, flagging them for investigation later, but mostly we're too overawed to do much as the minutes tick steadily by. No one wants to break the hush and I've taken the ship around in a full elongated loop before anyone does. I shut off Sim's music while we work and we're left in silence, alone in the cold expanse of the yawning dark with something glorious before us. The closer we get, the more detail is revealed. The more complex and intricate it all appears.

'Engines,' Kall declares at last. 'Go see if it's a boy-ship or a girl-ship.'

You can only take the boy out of the farm... I think as I pull the ship around, enjoying what faint press of manoeuvring the compensators permit.

Keeping well clear of the hulk – a steady kilometre above – I bring us over and across the rear section. Once we get there we're more puzzled than anything else. It's not a flat face but slightly convex and divided into perhaps a thousand small sections.

'Take us closer,' Kall urges, as though I'm not about to do that anyway.

It's not a view you often get of ships. Certainly not the big ones. There are redundancies built in of course, and the computers that run them are by several orders of magnitude smarter than the *Sak*'s AI, but anyone who's seen a spaceship has seen the power of their engines. Even here, it makes my skin slightly crawl to fly behind any sort of propulsion system.

Each of the small sections is circular and criss-crossed with lines. We can't see much more but Kall's cross-referencing the images just as fast as he can. Our records aren't exhaustive by any stretch of the imagination, but the ship can find nothing remotely similar.

I linger despite the sense of unease, reminding myself this thing has been dead for many millennia. We're not so far out that we've overlapped with an extant civilisation of this developmental level and not noticed. Nothing is going to start up and kick us into the next life.

Humanity reached the stars late, so we discovered once we got there. It was empty. No friendly faces, no helping hand to push us beyond the Sol system, just wreckage. There is life out there, some of it even sentient, but we're alone out in space. Of all those who had travelled the stars, by the time humans joined the club the others had died out or withdrawn.

One of the first sentient-inhabited planets humanity reached was a teeming agrarian economy. Burech, it's known by humans at least. The inhabitants live amid the ancient remains of a space-going civilisation, wholly uninterested by both their past and these fleshy aliens who tried to make contact. The accounts are mostly a series of frustrated refinements in contact approach – all good stuff in theory but it didn't work. Spaceships didn't impress them. Burechans seemed to know some of their history in space. They were one of the few species not to fall to societal collapse, but they'd moved beyond it all.

The scientists eventually helped themselves to what tech hadn't been melted down or tossed into volcanoes when they realised that the Burechans just didn't care. Anything with a circuit was without value and even that was an improvement on centuries of deep-rooted antipathy that had apparently gone before the present times.

Nowadays Burechans worship the seasons and the cycles of nature around them, but steadfastly ignore huge orbital stations visible from the surface. Of those only a few remain anyway, automated systems holding them in position until the day they can't anymore. Those become feast-days on Burech, celebrations of dramatic self-destruct protocols or using final power reserves to set course for their sun.

Humans still occupy monitoring posts on Burech, as custodians as much as picking over the remains. The other encounters have been generally more shocking, mostly for their one-sided nature. Most civilisations, most species, simply aren't there to learn from. Just their mistakes left behind – battlefields hanging in deep space, self-replicating technology gone feral, crumbling ruins of vast cities reclaimed by nature. Almost every expedition has brought back the same news.

No species endures for long. Some burn out, some are killed by their own creations. A handful like the Burechans realise their time in the stars is done and step away. The stark reality shocked many and changed the entire framework of planning. Now the rough consensus of policy among human-inhabited planets is designed not around the next ten years, but the next hundred. From the lessons learned by others, perhaps we'll do a little better.

'Next?' Sim asks me.

I glance back at the others. Three expectant faces are turned my way, all as eager as puppies, but they know it's my call. These things can be dangerous in a hundred different ways even though they're basically inert, empty lumps. And we still have some time. Even keeping a closer eye on us than normal, the company can't get anyone out here in the next few hours.

'Scans,' I tell them. 'Let's map this in detail and see what the computer can—'

I don't get to finish as Jad fairly screams, pointing at the screen.

'What?' I yell, scanning for threats. I can hear Kall doing the same, trying to work out if the ship's in danger but Jad hurls herself forward and grabs my shoulder, still pointing at the screen.

'A light!' she shouts loud enough to hurt my ear. 'There it goes again!'

She's right. It's tiny at this distance, but against the shadowed rear of the ship there's a short burst of white. It goes for a while then falls dark before coming again.

I've already thrown us backwards, emergency movement with all the small thrusters to wrench us away. Sim spins up the shields and manipulates them to the front as visions of missiles or other weaponry swim across my eyes. They're mostly for sub-space but may give us a chance to run. Before I can fire the main engines Jad needs to get back in her seat. I'm shouting orders but she's ignoring me, staring at the main screen with such crazed intent I hesitate.

'Computer, analyse!' she orders as I roar uselessly.

–analysing-pattern detected–

I freeze. Sim's sitting there with her mouth open.

'What pattern?' Jad demands.

–Fibonacci sequence-rapid burst-eleven steps-sequence repeated–

'Fib…' I tail off.

The full impact hits me. That's no random firing of light. That's no automated weapons array.

'Whispers of the great dark.'

That's something saying hello.

3

I'll admit, for a little while we panic. There's no running down the corridors, wailing or rending of clothes, but in all honesty my flight instructors wouldn't have been impressed with the useless shouting and general confusion.

"*Be the leader of the flight deck – the calm heart that drives the rest.*"

That's what they used to say in training. In space there's no time for chaos. Even these days with limited AIs in most ships, chaos is the fastest way to some dumb mistake that ends with you – briefly – remembering how inhospitable space is.

Finally I get myself together and the others calm down enough for me to pull us into a turn that's not going to bounce heads off consoles. A kick from the main engine and we get some distance between us and the winking hulk of a ship. Not far, but enough for me to think without being terrified we can't react to some automated defence system.

'That can't have been an accident, can it?' I say at last.

'Accident?' Simphiwe demands. 'Are you nuts?'

I raise my hands defensively. 'Just asking the question.

I'm freaking out here, see – this is my freaking out face! If it's a stupid question, fine, someone ask a better one. At the moment all I've got are wild conclusions and several thousand kilometres of run-up!'

Sim looks at me wide-eyed, but takes my point. 'None of us are systems techs,' she states, 'not high level ones anyway. And this is alien tech, so who knows what's possible?'

'Computer,' I call. 'Likelihood of that being a random firing of human-built systems?'

–excessive variables–

'Using random samples, below five per cent?'

–checking parameters-confirmed–

'Below one per cent?'

–confirmed-within margin of error–

'So at least we've got the stupid questions out of the way,' Sim comments. 'Come on, Song. You know contact theory well enough. Better than most of us I'm guessing. Mathematics is the most likely basis of first contact, of establishing any common principle or just demonstrating sentience.'

'Building a gigantic spaceship probably has that last bit covered already,' Kall mutters in the background. We ignore him.

'Computer,' I say. 'Recommended protocols for assessing possible sentient contact?'

–none–

'Oh thanks, helpful.'

'There's got to be something,' Sim says. 'Computer – protocols for first contact.'

–contact burst package in memory storage–

'But we don't know if that was contact or some random firing,' Jad says weakly, not even looking like she believes it herself.

'So what do we have to lose?' Sim asks. 'Ten minutes of looking stupid?'

'Fair point,' I accept. 'A few more minutes of that won't hurt us. So – we know there's some power here, the signal showed that. It's no great leap to there being some sort of power on a ship like that too. If we were damaged, our computer would either get us home or maintain systems as best it could for as long as it could, waiting for rescue. This could easily be primed to react to any sort of contact. Passive watching until we ran a scan and woke up something able to attract our attention.'

'That could also mean weapons are primed,' Kall warns. 'Whether or not they work after all this time.'

'Either way... do you want to head home? I didn't think so. Computer, prime contact burst package.'

–loading-primed–

'Send transmission.'

We all turn to the main screen, though of course there's nothing to see there. The contact burst package is a first-principles intro to talking to humans. It starts at the most basic level of maths and builds up from there – showing them a chunk of what we are, hopefully to the point where there's a basis to communicate. The problem is, we've never encountered a species with the computing power to read it properly. The theory works when we've encountered actual alien life, but it was done manually and took years. On a ship that size, you'd expect at least a limited AI to recognise it and start extrapolating in minutes.

'Do... do we just wait?' Sim asks.

'We could play a few hands of cards,' I say. 'Maybe we go investigate the breakfast bar?'

She gives me a slap on the arm. I stick out my tongue while, behind us, Kall votes for breakfast. I'm primed at the controls all the same. It's perfectly possible there's some sort of system running that might view a transmission as a hostile act.

The seconds drag by as I try to keep focus and not fidget, drip-drip-drip like some ancient torture. I can feel the adrenaline pumping through my body, excitement and terror playing merry havoc with my ability to think straight.

Finally I can't stand it any longer. The alien ship is doing nothing at all. There's no response, no acknowledgement. No signs of life or any cheap imitation of it. Just darkness and beauty. Maybe it was just a random firing of systems and the mathematical side is total coincidence. Maybe that's how their weapons are designed but the thing it tried to defend itself with broke fifty-thousand years ago?

Either way, just sitting there is pretty stupid.

I clear my throat. 'Kall, suit up and prep the shuttle. We're going over.'

The big man cheers while Sim raises an eyebrow. 'What happened to running a survey-scan?'

'We do that as well. Send the drones out – wait, just one to start with. Once it begins scanning, if nothing happens send more. Get the computer analysing any and all data as it comes in.'

'While you...?'

I smile. 'While I suit up. Got to be standing there to stake a claim, remember?'

'Assuming there's nothing alive there to contest your claim,' she counters.

I snort at that.

'The ship's ancient, just look at it. But you know the salvage laws and the company are expecting us at Venter Station. The ship will have reported the course change before we dropped out. I don't know whether they've buried sub-routines in it to tell them why as well, but either they know we've found something interesting or they assume we're pulling a fast one. Both mean the dispatch of a fast gunship and we've got less than twelve hours before we lose any salvage rights.'

Sim bites her lip then shrugs and starts preparing commands for the drone. She's not a part of my marriage nor witness to it, even if Jamal has suggested otherwise in the heat of the moment. Still, she's seen the corona of our arguments, felt the radiation of my anxiety tick steadily up. She knows I need a win here.

We've got twelve drones in total – no, actually eleven, given Sim drop-kicked one just before we left for reasons I never quite understood. They're a minor marvel of engineering so I wasn't exactly happy about that, but we seem to lose one on every trip. Usually because they're stuck inside a planet's atmosphere and don't have the fuel to escape.

I head to my room and quickly change into my flight suit; a white, chunky one-piece that makes me look like a stocky body-modder. Gel insulation bulks me out and the sensor tracks run from cap to toe with fifty-odd small connection studs. Most of the time we're just in normal clothes but a flight suit is designed to interface with an EVA rig. Halfway through I stop and sink down onto the bed. Suddenly I have full-on jitters, the momentous weight of... well everything. Life-changing out here is the flip-side of life-ending. I command the computer to bring up a vid-message on my wall and take a look at myself before I record anything. I don't look at my best if I'm honest. Silent dark, is it just my imagination or do I look old? More lines every year, more threads of grey in my hair.

I straighten myself out and try get presentable. The kids don't care, but on top of everything else I don't want to be looking like crap in front of Jamal. No time to wash though and I'm twitchy with anticipation – like I'm strung out on glitter-smoke.

Standing, I fit my arms into the suit and tell the computer to record. A blue icon appears on my screen and I turn left and right to let it get a better 3-D image, but when the red light appears I don't speak. I'm still wondering what to say. Finally I get a grip and smile for my loved-ones.

'Hi – a bonus message from your planet-hopping mum. We're due back at Venter Station soon. I'd hoped to get back early and give you a surprise but... well something's happened. A good something, I promise! The computer caught a signal fragment and we've found a wreck. The most beautiful, gigantic wreck I could ever have hoped to discover in a hundred lifetimes. I'm about to head over with Kall; do an initial check and record our claim. This... this really could be it. I don't want... damn, it's big! And I've never seen anything like it before! This could change everything for us. First there's an oddity I want to check out if I can and the formal claim to record of course. The detailed scan might give us what we need so I won't hang around, but...' I shrug. 'Or it could be nothing. A pile of junk interesting only to archaeologists. I won't know until we get out there. We could do with a break though, the rest of this trip has been an expensive bust. I need to file a claim and hope there's some decent salvage inside before the company arrive. As soon as they've got officials in the vicinity I'm classed as an employee and working on their behalf. A bonus in my pay packet rather than a percentage of the salvage value.

'Before I go out there, I just want to say I love you. All three of you. What I'm doing is dangerous, but I've got a good crew and, Jamal, this is why I bought the expensive EVA suit. To be safe as I do this and make it back to you all.

More soon. Be good to each other until I'm home, understand? Love you all.'

I finish up and get to dealing with the more intimate aspects a flight suit interfaces with, something my kids certainly don't need to see in a final message. That sorted I flag the vid for the computer to send and go find Kall.

The *Sakakawea* has two shuttles; two-person pods for short hops and escaping the ship in the event of disaster. By the time I reach the cargo bay Kall is already there and prepping the shuttle. His own flight suit is a more basic model, industrial grey with a ship's patch stuck over the breast. The shuttle hatch is open and I can see lights flickering inside as the computer runs diagnostics. My EVA suit is a great white lump taking up half of the compartment beside it. The other suits are reinforced mesh, grey and blue, with bulbous helmets and backpacks. Mine is closer to a medieval suit of armour, painted white. Which in some ways it is – half the pieces even have the same names. It's been customised to my spec of course to limit restrictions on my movement as much as possible, and while the mesh ones are tough, even at the flexible joints mine can take more of a battering.

Additional angular impact plates protrude at the extremities – shoulders, hips, knees, elbows – to take the worst, made lumpen by tiny manoeuvring jets embedded in them. Kall will have to wear a skeleton rig if he wants to do anything like that. The suit looks massive and threatening when you wear it. Arms bulky with a computer interface and coil gun harpoon, legs bearing tool compartments for a pry bar, cutting torch, claw, and expander. If it wasn't for the helmet lamps that I've always thought look like adorable little ears, it'd be a formidable prospect.

I've done this – wreck diving – five times before, excluding training. I've just never been the first into somewhere undiscovered. Or as the lead. Or unaware of what's waiting for me. There are a whole host of ways it can go wrong, but my EVA suit is a real tough beast for exactly that reason.

'Called the kids?' Kall asks as I enter. He's checking over his own EVA rig while the computer does mine. Kall's is just a standard survival model; basic systems and comms only. The bare minimum for surviving in the dark. I'll be doing any work that needs to be done while Kall watches from behind me and makes helpful comments, but there's safety in numbers.

I nod, too anxious and pumped to get the words out. I feel my hand tremble as I do, twitching in time with a rattling air-circ grate above my head.

'Help me with mine then,' he says with a smile. 'After that we'll get you into this beast. Shame you didn't buy one for all of us.'

'With the lecture I got about just buying one for myself? Jamal was not a happy bunny. Not without justification given it cost a year's rent, but...'

'But now both cost and telling-off are looking worthwhile, right?' Kall grins. 'All this needs is a grey paint job and decent weapons suite to make you a colonial marine!'

'Pretty sure there's an entry exam too!' I say, managing to laugh, 'but yeah, it makes me pretty bad-ass.' I tap the cylindrical attachment to the suit's right forearm. 'And this harpoon will put a hole in most things just as well as a pulse rifle.'

My suit is already open so once Kall is sorted with his I step directly in. I fit myself into the boots first, then gloves, then settle my backside in as I duck under the helmet.

'Here's hoping you've not put on weight,' Kall says with a chuckle before he taps a pad and the pieces begin to close up around me. I don't say anything. I'm more focused on the snug press on my body as I start to be encased in silvery-white. Inside the helmet a succession of green system lights scroll past my eyes as the flight suit nodes report a good contact.

'Computer, confirm comms link.'

–comms confirmed–

The EVA suit is a dead weight until I give the power order. I'd manage just a few steps on my own before needing a breather. But then the heaviness lifts and my limbs jerk with a new-found strength. With the suit on, I could toss Kall across the cargo hold. I see from the grin on his face he knows it.

'Ready?' he says through the comms link.

'Let's do this,' I reply and step out of the compartment.

The shuttle hatch is easily big enough for me to fit through and Kall just has to watch until I'm settled in the pilot's seat. Only then does he follow as I command the suit to release my visor and conserve stored air. Once Kall's in place I instruct the computer to close both hatches and we vent the remaining air around the shuttle. The sounds of the ship disappear almost entirely and I count down the seconds until we drop away into the void.

4

I love the shuttle. Maybe it's a pilot thing, maybe it's just me, but this little metal capsule is a whole lot of fun and, right now, that just amps up my excitement. As we drop away from the *Sakakawea,* I realise there's a grin plastered across my face. It's just as well I've got Kall with me. If Sim saw me like this, I'd not hear the end of it for a week.

I let us drift in the cool, silent darkness for a little while until the comms beeps into life.

'Comms check,' Sim says sharply in my ear, causing me to flinch. 'Song, you hearing me?'

'Yeah, I'm here. Why are you shouting?'

'Why are you just hanging there like you've forgotten which is the make-go-forward button?' she retorts, not unreasonably.

'She's letting me fly maybe?' Kall chimes in. The sound of his voice both beside me and on comms creates an odd, unearthly echo in my ear.

'Fat chance,' I say. 'Do more than beat out the dents you

put in the other shuttle and we'll maybe discuss it again. Maybe.'

I can hear music playing in the background again. That Sim's noticed me be a bit slow betrays a little anxiety, I realise. With the flight deck hers to command and call the tunes, she normally falls into a something akin to a trance. Building instructions for the drones, checking data and bumping it to the computer – it's all noise to me but she's born to it. The ship's scanners are nothing special but the first drone's already out and must almost be at the ship by now.

'I'm just waiting to see if that drone gets blown out the sky,' I lie.

'After someone's little lecture about how expensive drones are, I figured I'd keep it back. You go see if it's hostile instead. More cost efficient – for me at least.'

'Gee, thanks. You realise I've not left this ship to you in my will, right?'

'Don't worry, I was planning on seducing your husband. The kids are cute too. I'll probably keep them.'

I bite back a joke that would have sounded bitter and bitchy and instead engage the engine now that I'm well clear of the ship. It purrs as we leap forward, pressed back against our seats. The comms link is left open by unspoken consent. We're a talkative lot and when you get a few kilometres out in the great dark – in a shuttle barely four metres long – there's a real reassurance to hearing Sim tapping away, Jad muttering under her breath. The falling dark, that's what I call it. When up and down make no real sense, when you're at your most vulnerable your brain can switch. Make you feel like you're pitching head-first into the void, forever falling.

The shuttle glides towards the wreck, for a while

seeming to make no progress. Gradually it starts to loom on my main screen and the rear view shows the *Sakakawea* fading fast. Everything looks quiet. I can't see the drone I'm almost certain Sim did actually send, but I wouldn't expect to. The image isn't as good as on the flight deck, but just as I'm thinking it Sim clears her throat.

'I'm sending you a better picture, okay?'

'It's like you're right here in my head, hon.'

She chuckles. 'Oh Song, not in front of the children!'

For a while nothing happens, then the *Sakakawea*'s computer fires a packet of info at the shuttle and improves my view – sharing some of what Sim can see. That magnificent sight returns. Sunlight licking the gold and silver streaks that stand bright against the battered black hull.

'First a close-up look at where we saw the light,' I comment, easing the shuttle towards the rear of the alien ship. 'After that... well, there are plenty of ways in.'

'Most of which won't be safe.'

'Don't be such a nag,' I chide her. 'You'll make the youngster worry.'

That makes Kall snort, but he sensibly doesn't rise to the taunt.

I urge the shuttle on a little faster, keen to be done, but as we close on the wreck I experience a flutter of trepidation. It's vast – that much was clear before, but up close I'm just a speck against its side. Without thinking about it I slow the drive as we come up to it, feeling more than a little like some idiot in a dingy rowing towards two thousand metre high cliffs.

Fortunately there's no current to drag me forward and I can hold position with ease. We sit in the shadow of the wreck, its bulk blocking out the sun so effectively I can barely see a halo of light. Up close the strange network that patterns most of the rear face still makes no damn sense to me. Those thousand-odd depressions are circular with a broad cross-hatch of metal over each, maybe twenty metres across and five deep. I could fit the shuttle inside one if I could get it through the cross-hatch, which I've no intention of doing.

'Sim, can you roll back the image of the light?'

'Hold on.'

I hang in space, listening to her tap the controls. I've got a rough idea of where it came from, but I can see nothing to guide me now. I switch on the searchlight and play it around. Nothing jumps out at me, neither literally nor figuratively. There's no obvious damage to this section I realise. I don't know how their propulsion systems work, but on human ships you always target the engines in battle. Here the damage is elsewhere.

'Who does that?' I wonder aloud.

'Huh?' Sim replies, clearly focused on her task.

'Just thinking – what was on this ship that they didn't try to destroy it? It looks like they were boarded. There was something here the attackers wanted.'

'And they probably found it,' she drawls. 'This all happened tens of thousands of years ago. Plenty of time for whoever attacked to come back. Finish the job.'

'True.'

I feel a burst of childish disappointment all the same, but before long my screen zooms out of its own accord. Sim's controlling it from the flight deck, panning back until a highlighted section appears in my view. I put the shuttle into a corkscrew turn to bring us up to the correct section. It's a circular depression just like all the others. No waving alien sat inside, no apparent entryway to the ship. There's nothing that I can see on first glance, but I do a careful sweep with the searchlight all the same.

'Wait, what's that?' Jad calls.

She dots the screen with a marker at a point where the cross pieces of the metal grid meet. I nudge the ship left and then hold position, squinting forward at what she's seen. Then I feel stupid and zoom the view.

I gasp in unison with the others. There is something different about this section, but it's subtle. Artfully done. There's a cut-out section here, something the others don't have as I turn to compare. A circular section maybe a metre wide – almost indistinguishable from the rest but Sim cycles through the screen views and the discrepancy becomes clear. This was the source of the light – hidden against the dark metal but in fact it's some sort of glass disc set in the hull.

'Weird. This has been deliberately put here, but why?' I wonder.

'For a good reason,' Sim replies. 'Just don't expect that reason to make sense to a human mind or even apply for the last fifty-thousand years.'

I nod. The temptation is to forget none of this was done for our benefit. Rescue protocols, rules of engagement, logic – whatever it was behind this decision, it's literally alien to us and long-gone.

'What about that?' Kall says. 'Look, below it.'

I zoom further. It's small but something has been engraved beneath the glass disc – three flattened ovals that remind me of something. One is plain, another is filled with crosshatch markings with a thick line down the centre. The middle one combines them, like a cat's eye with cross-hatches on either side of a lenticular centre.

'That's officially weird,' I comment. 'Anyone recognise it? Mathematical maybe?'

No one comes up with a clever suggestion. Or even a stupid one for that matter; we're all stumped. I rack my brain for anything it might mean, but even when Sim gets the computer to run a comparison she finds nothing of interest.

After another check of the section and its surroundings I run out of patience. Drone information is coming in as the small sensor craft begin sweeping the wreck's exterior. Nothing surprising yet, just filling in the map – adding detail to what we can see of the vast bulk. With something so big it's going to take hours to scan the entirety in any serious way, but Sim sent one or two to investigate the central section where the most basic scan has brought up multiple openings. We're working on the assumption they're shuttle bays of various kinds – on a ship this size there are likely multiple transport hangars.

Close to those are small open sections, many displaying weapons damage. From the number, size, and fact they seem to have been targeted, Sim's provisionally flagged them as fighter-bays or escape pods. Either way it took a battering beyond anything I want to fly near, the guts of the wreck torn open and exposed to the light. More significantly, the drones scanning that part detected power running inside the ship. Not a lot and the hull's surface seems to scramble or block sensors, but something. Some latent system waiting for command or mindlessly working to keep the wreck's orbit from decaying.

Looking at the damage, it's clear there's nothing organic alive in there. No community surviving generation after generation in there – not for so long. Further up there's a large, damaged section – a huge tear in the hull that'd fit almost any human-built ship I've ever seen. Nothing survives damage like that and it's not the only ship-killing impact the initial scan has brought up. Even hoping for some species that's devolved to primitive levels as background systems keep them alive... there's just no chance. But if there's anything with the capacity to run power it's both exciting and dangerous.

I bring the shuttle around and head to the nearest of the shuttle bays at the middle section. It's two kilometres away – not far in a shuttle except the whole way there I'm skimming the ravines, peaks, and valleys of an ancient spaceship. I've done similar in a flyer back home, strictly in atmosphere though since the pilots who go asteroid skimming are just insane. Even with surface scans it's too easy to meet a surprise, but here I'm keeping a sensible altitude without ruining all the fun.

'Enjoying yourself?' Kall asks. He looks less comfortable when I glance over, squashed into his seat and gripping the console.

'Immensely,' I reply, but as soon as I speak I have to throttle back and bring it around so we're facing the shuttle bays.

'Now – what do we have here?'

There are three bays from what I can see, broad with rounded sides. One open, one mostly closed and one buckled inward, a great spread of amorphous metal tangles jutting out from below. It looks like a fifty metre stretch below this part of ship is missing by the awkward line of the hull. What is there has been bitten out and heat-fused by something. Sharp cables, beams and struts all protrude well beyond the main impact zone and I keep clear. To get closer would be to risk the shuttle.

'Ah, anyone else getting a weird feeling about this?' I ask.

'What do you mean?'

'The oval bays. Remind you of anything?'

'Those shapes by the light,' Sim says after a moment's pause. 'Whispers of the dark, do you think?'

'They had to be there for a reason. Why not this? The light attracts our attention, directs us to a certain entrance.'

'But why?'

'Like you said earlier, probably for a good reason fifty-thousand years ago. Now? Probably none, but if you were stranded here and desperately waiting for assistance, you might want to direct rescuers to the safest entrance or the closest one to where survivors are.'

'Why put the light way out back then?'

'I don't have an answer for that one. Maybe it fits some sort of standard operating procedure?'

'One open, one almost closed, one basically not there anymore,' Sim muses as though she's working through a schoolroom puzzle. 'Could be a clue I guess.'

'Either way, I was heading into door number one anyway,' I add.

'Makes me suspicious,' Kall says.

'Of what? Long-dead aliens?'

'Of everything. It's weird and—'

'And nothing,' I butt in. 'We've got a job to do.'

'But this isn't it,' Kall argues.

I bite my lip. 'When that job pays better, I'll pass up golden opportunities, okay?'

'Wait a minute,' Sim replies on his behalf. 'Kall's got a point. Hold position and let me at least check it out.'

'Fine.'

From my screen I see a shape moving up behind me – a blue dot indicating a drone. It arrives in almost exactly a minute, close enough that I wonder whether she'd actually done it deliberately, but Sim says nothing as the drone slows in front of me then drifts towards the open bay.

They're bulbous-nosed grey lumps, a metre long and dully functional. There's a blunt comms spike close to the front between frog-eye lamps that can be raised and turned. A tow-line is hidden in the belly too, in the event of shuttle malfunction.

It activates lights as it moves across the threshold and starts to play them around the shuttle bay. Fifty metres wide and a little less high. I zoom in my view and see... not a lot. The drone starts to ping back data but that doesn't add much. The bay is empty; of ships, wreckage and pretty much everything else. There are protrusions that look like repair cradles, an oval bank that probably was a control section and not a lot besides.

Then the drone updates its scans and I see there are panels everywhere. No doubt they conceal more, but there's no power so far as the drone can detect. I drum my fingers on my control deck, but here Sim's in control so I just have to wait until she gives me the okay. The ship's computer feeds me what she's doing, but my shuttle can't do the job nearly as well.

'Looks boring,' I say. 'Just how we want it, right?'

'There,' she says, ignoring me. 'Exit. Damage to one side, it's broken or propped open.'

'Can you get the drone inside?'

'Probably, but it may struggle. I'm just flagging it for you. You've got suit-drones on that fancy rig of yours don't you?'

'Only two. It's not military stock.'

We wait. It's agony sitting there doing nothing – so close to the prize. Finally the drone's finished its scan of the interior and the computer's running through the intricate details. Sim's already checked the headlines and it's pretty much what we expected.

'Clear of debris,' she reports. 'Minimal small particles, minor obstacles. No power, unknown composites in the walls and signs of mechanisms on all surfaces. Nothing that should stop you going in, Song.'

'Side-note,' Jad pipes up. 'Nothing about the ship, but it's about to get dark in there.'

I peer forward at the unlit cavity ahead of me.

'It's already pretty dark,' I point out. 'What with us being out in space and all.'

'Yeah – more so. The orbit of the ship is taking it around the planet. Nothing unusual, just thought I'd mention it. Entering shadow in one minute.'

'Plunged into cold and darkness. However will I cope?'

'Like she wouldn't whine if it had come as a surprise,' Sim mutters in the background.

'I heard that!'

'Oh. Whoops. I must have forgotten how a comms system works. Deary me.'

'You know, on some ships they have a little respect for the captain. Even call them "Captain" from time to time.'

'Only to their faces,' Sim reassures me. 'Behind their back it's something else. Happy to start that whenever you want, boss-lady.'

I harrumph but the conversation's going nowhere and I have places to be. I ease the shuttle forward, ready at a moment's notice to fire the direction engines and jolt me back out if necessary. As it is, nothing happens. The shuttle glides gently forward. The drone's lights play briefly across me then return to the interior of the bay.

The walls are pale matte grey, the floor a darker shade presumably to help orient the eye. Not that there is a "down" right now, not without power in the place. But the nominal floor is smooth while there are ridges and projections on the walls and ceiling almost like climbing aids.

Smears of dust adorn sections or hang like ghosts in the air, given brief life by the play of our lamps, but mostly the bay is clean and clear. No weapon impacts scar the walls, no ancient blood stains the floor. It's just dark and cold and full of sadness somehow.

Honestly I don't know what I expected. I've read a few accounts of investigating battle-damaged wrecks, but I don't remember the details well. We know there have been a number of system-spanning conflicts of genocidal proportions, have even come across battlefields but those are just a huge mess of debris that's barely worth the salvage. Actual battle-damaged craft you can explore are incredibly rare. Most lose their orbits and crash if they're not destroyed entirely, leaving little of use for people like me. So maybe after a hundred thousand years in space there wouldn't be brains splashed on the walls anyway. Somehow the question's never come up in my life until now.

It's a functional place on first assessment. The smooth edges of panels and units remind me faintly of a human style of ship-building, but one you don't see in these parts much. The sleek Aratan craft are the closest I can imagine, but those are mirror-polished and knife-shaped. This is... well, functional but with a smooth near-organic grace to everything. It makes the *Sakakawea* look blockish and dull in comparison. I make a mental vow to convert her with whatever this gold and black material is – honour the ship that has made my fortune. And with that in mind...

'Bringing her down,' I comment as I put the shuttle on the nominal floor.

The suckers flash orange on my console for a moment

then turn green to indicate they've got a secure hold. I check everything, glance over at the drone that's just hanging in space a few yards away and slowly directing its lights around the bay.

'Close visor,' I say, to my suit as much as Kall. He has to do it manually, but after a few seconds it's secured in place and he gives me a thumbs-up.

'Opening shuttle.'

My EVA suit confirms it's ready and I pull the atmosphere from the shuttle before opening the top hatch. A tap on the seat-release frees me from the straps and tilts it so I can get out. Kall's nimbler, easing himself over the edge and swimming through the zero-g space until he's clear. I work my bulky frame out of the hatch and close it up behind me.

That done I can get my boots onto the floor. They clunk heavily onto the metallic surface. A dial spins briefly on my Heads-Up-Display as the suit searches for a good balance then it flashes green and I take a step. It's laboured, but no different to walking on muddy ground and I cross the bay quickly to peek outside. Kall drifts up behind, grabbing my shoulder to anchor himself before seeking a boot lock.

Far into the distance, blazing bright even with the suit compensating, the last of the sun peeks around the planet's edge.

'Nightfall,' I comment, 'and all's well.'

'Better'n well,' Kall says. 'We're about to be rich.'

'Let's not be hasty on either front,' Sim replies. 'Now get out of the way so I can pull the drone back.'

'Worried about the cost again?'

'Just want it in position in case the signal weakens,' she says. 'That hull material could be a problem so we might have to relay comms. Don't want you to fall dark.'

I shiver and nod, searching for the *Sakakawea* amid the starry darkness, but I can't make it out at that distance.

'You know what's odd about this?' I ask, turning to Kall. 'There's no writing.'

I point towards what I'd expect to be a console in a human equivalent ship. It's entirely blank – without texture or colour. That bit isn't a surprise, but all human ships have notifications and warnings in every working section.

'Maybe a hundred thousand years ago they didn't believe in regulations and safety notices,' he says with as much of a shrug as is possible in a suit.

'A species that built something this big?' Sim chimes in. 'Seems unlikely.'

'And yet there's nothing,' I say. 'No permanent writing of any kind. It's not insane, just a little odd to my mind.'

'Enough wasting time,' Sim replies. 'Do it already.' Her words are echoed by Jad and Kall claps his hands like a child.

'Yes, Miss. Signal clear?'

'Signal clear,' she confirms.

'Good. In which case – my name is Song Ezaralar, captain of the scout ship *Sakakawea,* registered in Thieler Port of my home planet, Sien Nau. We have discovered a wrecked ship of unknown but non-human origin and on behalf of myself and my registered crew I claim it under the Interplanetary Salvage Agreement. As per my contract of employment with the Filerich Conglomerate, I offer them sole and exclusive partnership rights in this enterprise.'

There's a small cheer in the background from Jad and Kall as Sim taps away on her console.

'Declaration transmitted to all necessary figures,' she reports, by which she means three planetary councils, our employers and a handful of lawyers – spreading the word far enough that no corporate arsehole suggests in a board meeting it's cheaper to murder us and take the find for themselves.

I don't work for particularly murderous types, of course. Not compared to some anyway. Still – the day you start trusting in the morals of management is the day you get blown up in some distant backwater by a bastard with share options. Across my view I see the light fade as the sun disappears. I'm still looking out at the vastness of space when a panel on the ceiling briefly glows. Without warning the shuttle bay doors slide shut.

5

I don't move. I don't scream. I don't even speak for a few seconds. I simply stare at those dark slabs of metal and fail to understand what's going on. Then it hits me like a punch to the gut and I feel the wind go out of my lungs. Somewhere distant, Kall is yelling. A wall of noise; jagged panic that fades as quickly as it comes. Then he falls silent and all I can hear is the gasp of his breath.

'Sim?'

I hear my voice without recognizing it and somehow jump at the sound. My heart pounds at my chest, rattling against the ribs while a rushing noise fills my ears. For a moment I stagger, the wreck jolting around me like it's being struck by ordinance. There is no right-way-up here though, no angle from which the universe makes more sense. I flail briefly then submit, the boot-lock on the surface below enough to root me.

'SIM!' I yell now, panic catching up with shock. 'Anyone?'

No response. No sound at all, just my own desperate panting filling my ears. And now I'm truly scared. Ice-cold, in-the-bone terror. We're all alone in a tomb with just a few blades of light holding the darkness at bay. I feel a lurch in my stomach, like I'm on the edge of a precipice.

Kall lumbers over to the great door and I follow – trying to run, but the suit only permits a laboured stamp. Thumping our fists on it does exactly nothing but I can't help myself. Terror is a wild animal inside me now; clawing, screeching, frantic to escape. Kall is raging, curses I've never heard him utter before.

'Sim! Jad! Computer!'

–yes–

I whirl around, too confused by fear to think straight, but of course the sound has come from my ear rather than behind me. Still I find myself staring at the shuttle as the drone continues to dumbly trace a repeating pattern around the empty shuttle bay with its lights.

'Computer!' I repeat. 'Can you hear me!'

–yes–

'What's happened?' Kall breaks in.

–comms link severed-unknown cause–

I look at him, seeing my own confusion mirrored in his face. 'Unknown? Wait – how are... oh hells, you're not the *Sakakawea* are you?'

–correct–

'Shit!'

The fear returns. I'm not in contact with the ship, just a small sub-section that resides in the shuttle. Normally it's linked to the ship itself so there's no difference, but it's far more limited on its own.

'We're on a void-damned wreck,' Kall says. 'It's thousands of years old. How can the door have shut on us?'

'Wait, Kall – shut up a second. Computer – you said unknown cause. Isn't it the hull of this ship?'

–negative-comms link severed prior to activation of bay doors–

'How?'

–signal disruption-unknown method-unknown source–

'But that's...'

I gape at Kall. I don't know how to finish that sentence. Even the attempt could lead me down paths that leave me a gibbering wreck. The implications break over me like an ocean wave. My head swims and it's a while before I can even think straight, but there's a voice at the back of my head that's screaming for attention.

'What are we going to do, Song?' Kall asks pitifully. 'Captain – what's happening?'

'I've no idea,' I admit, though I can see it's the last thing the big man wants to hear. For all his size, he's young and has led an orderly life. He trusted that I knew what I was doing when I came in here. Didn't once wonder at my rush. Didn't once think there might be a risk of something like this happening.

Nor did I, I remind myself. *This is... I've never heard of anything like this. There's no action plan here.*

'No time to cry, Song,' I declare like a mantra. 'Shit shit shit – right, training, come on, what do you do? AIM, yes, that's it. Assess – Itemize – Manage.'

I've trained for this, or rather for accidents but it's all the same really. Days of drilling for moments of terror in a wreck. Unless you're an idiot with a death wish, you get certified in wreck diving before you try it even under supervision. Space will kill you if you let it. Any number of things can result in disaster and then you're on the clock. Falling dark isn't the worst of them, but normally that's just a comms breakdown.

'Aim?' Kall returns to pounding on the bay door and I have to yell at him to get him to stop.

'Shit – Kall, stop that. You can't break it down! Stop or you'll tear your suit!'

I'm screaming at him, but he doesn't seem to hear me. I have to grab him by his arm and almost haul him away from the door, which is dangerous enough as it is. My powered suit could rip his open just as easily as he might damage it on the door by himself, but I'm careful and it breaks his rhythm. He turns, hands raised as though ready to fight, but the wild look in his eyes isn't violent. Only confused and desperate.

'Stop,' I repeat. 'Stand still and listen to my voice. We're going to get out – I promise you that, just... give me a moment to think.'

He gives me an uncomprehending look but finally nods and lowers his hands.

'Right – now, "Assess",' I gasp, flailing to focus for a moment. 'The doors have shut. Ah...'

I look around. For a moment I don't see anything but darkness and dead, grey metal. My helmet lights scour the walls only to be frustrated at every sweep. No malevolent face peers back at me, no blinking of a malfunction or security response. It could be a stone crypt rather than a marvel of engineering.

'No panels, no lights, no obvious mechanism. Comms are down, not caused by the hull. We're shut in and not getting out that way.'

'Now "Itemize". We're healthy. Suits are both intact, shuttle and drone likewise. Air reserve is good. Computer – confirm condition of suit air scrubbers.'

–optimal-reserve tank at maximum–

'System check?'

–all systems operational–

'Do you have control of the drone?'

–confirmed–

'Right then.' I give Kall an encouraging grin that hardly fits my state of mind, but it seems to lessen his panic. 'Next – "Manage". Manage the problem. Whether it's a random system firing or some sort of intruder alert, there's no way we break out of an external door. What we can't do is stay here.'

'Why not? Won't the *Sak* come looking for us?'

'Of course – but they've only got one maintenance drone. It'll take a long time to cut through that door.'

I look at the bay's only exit. There's no way the shuttle is fitting through that, but the drone might.

'Computer, assign direct control of drone to my pad.'

–assigned–

'What are you doing?' Kall asks but I ignore him for the moment.

I flip up a panel on my forearm and a projected screen lights up. I've only used the remote access once in my life, but in theory I should have full access to the drone's capabilities. It's a little fiddly to use in an EVA suit, my armoured fingers aren't exactly dextrous. Still, this is an emergency and I'll make do.

'Computer, clone your AI to the drone.'

–warning-exceeds recommended parameters–

'Will it be unable to function?'

–some functions may be inhibited-scan data will be purged–

'I'll take that risk, no wait. Send exterior scan to my suit and map location, then override warning.'

–complying-complying-completed–

'Good. If the doors open for any reason, take the shuttle outside and signal the *Sakakawea.* If the ship's computer estimates the shuttle can effectively obstruct the door, do that and attempt to signal us.'

–acknowledged–

'Good. First of all, Kall, let's look at that door. See if there's anything to be done there before we abandon it. Drone, scan the door for override or manual controls.'

–scanning–

It drifts silently to the doors, lights playing over the metal while the scan progresses. It directs me to one section above where the doors meet. There's a small blank panel, slightly raised from the rest, about thirty centimetres square. I prod at that a while, trying to see if it's an interface or cover panel, but the thing appears rigid and inert.

Taking the pry bar from my leg, I work at it but can get no purchase. My anxiety turns quickly to anger and I raise the pry bar like a spear instead. One thump doesn't do much but the second dents whatever metal it's made of. That gives me a thin opening, just enough to get the bar in and while I can't make much headway, it moves a little.

Buoyed, I get my cutter out and use the fearsome power of those shears to chop an ugly tear in the covering plate. A bit more work and I've exposed something underneath – I don't recognise what, but there are indentations that could be ports or power terminals. Kall fetches a hard line from the shuttle, having to disengage the locks holding it down first so he can drag it over. There's no guarantee this will work at all, but if there's any similarity in mechanisms, the computer might be able to rig something.

I jam the mouth of the cable into the ragged hole and instruct the shuttle computer.

'Computer, engage connection.'

I feel the cable squirm and wriggle under my hand as it shifts and probes obscenely. Designed to interface with anything, it'll mould itself to whatever it finds and jam a few dozen metal feelers into crevices, trying to configure some sort of connection. I have to wait a while before it's finished. Any human-made port it'll work out some sort of link in a few seconds, but I've no idea if this is indeed even related to the door control.

–insufficient connection– the computer reports, unsurprisingly.

'Override all protocols,' I reply. The most half-arsed bodge is more than I can even hope to achieve here. 'Provide power to any possible connection.'

–exceeding parameters–

'Command override. Disregard possible damage except to myself. Attempt all possible options to open bay door.'

–complying-complying-attempt failed-unknown connection type-non-responsive–

'Shit.'

We're quiet for a while. I had almost allowed myself to hope but clearly that was a stupid idea and Kall looks similarly defeated. However remote a possibility that feeding power in might trigger the door, it was my best idea and it's failed.

'Okay,' I say finally and straighten up. 'We really can't stay here any longer.'

'You think we're in danger?'

'Oh we're in danger,' I assure him. 'I just don't know what sort. Any sort of degraded system with power could be dangerous, just as old equipment or structural damage can kill if you don't know what it is.'

I grip the cable and am about to pull it out when I stop. The shuttle's in position if the door does open somehow and I'm not taking it with me otherwise. It's too big to fit through the other exit so there really is no point when we're just going to abandon it.

'You've failed us shuttle,' I say with forced humour. 'Now you can just hang there and think about what you've done until we get back here with the salvage crew, understand?'

The computer doesn't respond of course. Even if it had twigged I was talking to it, its conversation skills aren't great at the best of times. I take a deep breath and wave Kall towards the only exit remaining to us. The doorway that leads further inside this wreck – precisely where I don't want to go without a full salvage team by my side. Or for preference, slightly ahead of me.

I try to summon the spirit of exploration that first moved the younger me to train as a space pilot, but it's gone. Maybe I left it outside those bay doors. Wherever it went, the older me just feels scared and lacking any sort of spirit. With no other options and Kall in the more easily-damaged suit, I go through.

6

I send the drone on ahead of me of course. It moves in tiny increments through a short passageway, just a few centimetres clearance on either side. The drones aren't built to manoeuvre through enclosed spaces. In no atmosphere it moves with a creepy, juddering silence.

'I'm an idiot,' I mutter as I watch it.

'What?' Kall replies, sounding anxious when normally he'd be cracking a joke.

I turn to him as I speak and realise he's even more freaked out than me. I'm going to have to be a proper captain now. He's got no experience of this, just has the standard extra-vehicular time under his belt. Fixing the *Sak*, not entering a derelict unknown place.

'Bugs,' I explain. 'My suit has two mini drones.'

I command the suit to confirm their status then order it to release both mini drones from their housings over each scapula. Triangular and roughly the size of my palm, they don't have the power or range of the main drones, but they're perfect for a wreck like this.

I don't feel anything as the suit complies, but almost

immediately a pair of lights flick on from behind me so I order them forward. The bugs follow the drone through and automatically start scanning the space they find themselves in, feeding information back to my suit where it's overlaid onto my faceplate.

Once through the narrow section the larger drone increases its lights. There's a large space beyond the doorway, a hangar I imagine. It looks cluttered. I can't see well in the dark of course, even with my HUD able to enhance the view. With the lights and texture maps from the three drones however, I can make out a tangle of wreckage about twenty metres ahead. There's more beyond, the drones steadily filling in an initial basic outline. The unidentifiable mess makes me nervous, but I shouldn't waste too much time.

Predictably, nothing leaps out to smash any of the drones. I receive an image of a large space, maybe ten times the volume of the shuttle bay, described in ghostly overlay. I look around at the skeletal lines of gantries, seeing little more when I enter the passage and get the benefit of our various lights. There are three levels on each side, great lumps of ripped and twisted metal dotting the space. Some are tethered, others hang still in the air. There's a similarity to some of the pieces; sharp, narrow prows with a bulbous body. If they were human-built I'd say they were unmistakably short-range fighters. As it is, all I'm certain of is they've been smashed up with savage violence. There are pieces everywhere plus shattered wall panels, all looking like signs of weapon impacts.

'Definitely looks like they lost the fight.' Kall comments, peering past me.

'Against whom though?' I wonder. 'A boarding engagement like this is done in armoured suits and I don't see anything like that here.'

There's a whole mass of material inside there, but nothing with the shape to suggest a biological entity. Nothing in the scan conforms to anything I could imagine there, but how would I even know what I was looking for?

Once the drones have a good picture of the hangar, I identify the exits and try to map them onto the outside view I'd had – mere minutes and half a lifetime ago. I get the drone to confirm that then duck through the doorway that's almost level with my eye line. Just stepping out makes me want to wet myself with fear. I've no idea what's there, but some part of this ship is aware of my presence. Through the gloom of this mausoleum, it could be watching me right now and I'd never see it coming.

I check the harpoon built onto my right arm. It's a bulky piece of kit with bolts stowed on either side. I prime and load one – not knowing if I'm being stupid or not, but the reassurance of that grapple-tip protruding over the back of my gauntlet gives me a scrap of courage.

'Why are you doing that?' Kall asks fearfully.

'Just to be safe.'

'Safe from what?'

'From...' I pause. 'Honestly? Just to make myself feel better about wandering about in the dark.'

'Oh.'

Checking the map I see that we have to cover about a hundred metres, down the near side of the hanger. There's debris in the way, but nothing we can't easily bypass. It's a straight run, nothing obviously dangerous about it.

–electromagnetic field detected– the drone reports suddenly.

Once I finish jumping out of my skin, I take a second

look around. I can't see anything new so I consult the map of the room. A yellow marker indicates the EM field it's found – a trace of some electrical system running. Obviously there was something that shut the doors in the shuttle bay, but it was too minimal or shielded to detect. Here, the drone's caught something more obvious.

It's across the hangar though, the no-man's land of debris that I don't want to cross for anything. As I look at the map a second pings up – alongside the first. They look like doorways – to what I can't tell, but there's some electronic system running there.

'Shit shit shit shit,' I mutter. 'Do we need to go and look?'

'What? Why?' Kall demands. 'Let's leave anything with power well alone!'

I rack my brains, trying to work out the correct choice, but I realise I can't think straight right now. I'm still too freaked out by the whole situation to do anything beyond follow my wreck-diving training. There, investigating any signs of tech is the whole point of the dive, the treasure that could make us all rich.

The whole reason for coming here is to stake a claim, to find something that'll mean I'm not some washed-up bankrupt failing to hold on to her kids. There's something gone weird in this wreck though, some systems still running and acting erratically. I realise I don't give a damn at this point. Whether or not the claim notification was sent, I just want to get out. If I can escape through the other shuttle bay, I'll do that, but I've already had one close on me. Do I need to see what sort of systems are still running here before we can risk making a break for it?

As though trying to help my decision, there's a rogue stutter of light overhead – nothing bright, just a greenish glow that starts to run down a part of the ceiling only to meet some sort of obstacle. The two forces edge back and forth for a second then one wins out and the light vanishes.

I shiver as best I can inside the suit and Kall moans briefly in fear. The systems are all messed up in this wreck. It's a miracle anything works at all, but now it's hidden from the most likely back-up energy source, the sun, any firings are likely to be even more fitful.

Didn't a wise man say never look back? It doesn't matter if you're running from something or toward something, so long as you're running. Time to leave this place.

'Let's go,' I say in what I hope is a firm voice.

I start off, slow and careful steps, trusting Kall to keep close behind. The large drone maintains a steady ten metres ahead while I send the bugs down the far end. They all continue to search methodically around with their lights, checking for obstacles. And if I'm honest, also hopefully making themselves more of a target if there is any automated security system left here.

There are a few more flickers of light across the hangar. Enough to make us both jump, but I can't see anything in this light. I've seen this movie – this is when the ghost appears from nowhere behind us. Part of me wants to turn and check, part of me doesn't. Everything goes dark again but it doesn't stop my imagination which is in overdrive.

'Shit, Song, get a grip!' I mutter in the privacy of my own suit.

Somehow it's a comfort that there's no atmosphere. I could scream and shout as much as I like, the sound isn't going anywhere outside my suit aside from through the comms link.

Best you don't scream, I remind myself. *You might send Kall right over the edge.*

Just that little moment of practicality does the trick. It

snaps me back to my senses and I feel the tension in my chest ebb just a little.

Panic won't help, I remind myself, weirdly hearing it in the calm, firm voice of my primary school teacher, Mx Arturo. *You're in trouble here, this is dangerous. You've got no time for being stupid and seeing ghosts.*

I pause. The little voice at the back of my head suggests I'm tempting fate, but while there must have been tens of thousands of dead here, they're long gone. Even if ghosts were real, I tell myself, energy dissipates. It's a miracle anything is left and while the computer wasn't able to date this wreck with any semblance of accuracy, it's ancient. Any residual soul or energy that isn't being charged by the sun itself, would have faded into nothing tens of thousands of years ago.

Also, ghosts aren't real. Don't forget that bit.

The grips on the walls here are more pronounced. I stop and take one – it seems solid, but when I pull it towards me it slides a short way out of the wall. Fully extended it looks even more like a climbing aid of some sort. There's a regularity to the shapes, an indent in the centre of the hand-hold with thicker, upturned edges. It doesn't fit my hand well, but I can grip it to test if I can use the network to bypass a lumpen block of metal in my path.

The block is maybe two metres high. We can go round it but the left-hand-side has been opened and looks eviscerated. Fat cables, wires and angular metal limbs spill haphazardly out. From a distance it looks like a huge spider waiting in ambush for something to pass, but up close it's clearly just some machine catastrophically damaged.

Disengaging my boots, I let my body drift up while using the hand-holds to guide me over. Kall watches me then follows once I'm over. The drone is already past. It waits silently at the entrance to the next shuttle bay. There the door is open, inviting me in. As I reach it there's another stutter of light above us. It ends as quickly as the first did but to my faint horror it's accompanied by flashes of yellow and pink inside the bay.

'Drone, stop in the doorway,' I order in a fit of paranoia. 'Right at the top.'

'What are you doing?' Kall asks, his voice sounding cracked but perhaps it's just the comms playing up.

'Just being stupidly cautious,' I reassure him. 'We'll need to crouch to get through, but I've just watched one door close on me.'

The bugs zip through the remaining gap ahead of me before I get ready to creep through under the drone. The drones illuminate a fair chunk of the bay ahead as I hesitate, but nothing happens. There's no movement or anything. Maybe it is just random firings, a system malfunction that happens every time the wreck passes into shadow and it loses the power source.

'Drone, systems check,' I say while shuffling past it. Just making sure, I tell myself.

–all systems nominal–

The shuttle bay is a real mess. So much so I struggle to make it all out as the various lights cast interlocking shadows. Smashed equipment, console banks, the remains of a shuttle too most likely. It's hard to tell now, almost half of the entire bay is broken. The wall to my left and much of the ceiling have been punched inwards. Metal supports protrude like ribs after something has ripped its way out of a body and there's a heat-fused mess of... well, something, partially embedded in the floor.

Kall whistles at the destruction as he follows me in. From the centre of the room we get a better view of the adjoining bay too. The shared wall is half gone, but there's no escape for us in that direction. Just a maze of sharp angles and bay doors that have been crushed inward and subjected to incredible temperatures. I can see the heat scarring in this bay too. However it happened, the worst of the impact was taken by the adjoining wall before it burst apart.

'Shit,' Kall adds once he takes it all in. 'Impact damage. Heat damage. This place saw a whole variety of weaponry going off.'

I nod. Everything in the room is junked, including the outer door mechanism in this bay it appears. One of the doors has stopped before fully closing, the other is fully shut but buckled inward. More importantly I can see blessed starlight through the gap. It's not a lot, less than a metre, but enough to ease my bulky EVA suit through. 'Almost there,' I say to myself as I check the room. I'm making no mistakes now. I'm getting Kall out and myself home to my family. Everything else can sort itself out however the universe fancies. If it means some shitty planet-bound job right now I don't care, but there are a multitude of dangers in this shuttle bay. To cross it won't be hard, but it's worth a check.

The drone drifts silently past me, light playing around the bay and showing even more of the brutal treatment it's received. The walls are more textured, a small forest of protrusions extended anywhere from a few centimetres to almost a metre into the room. What flashed with light I can only guess at, but there is one main arc-shaped bank that looks least damaged. It's dark now, nothing obvious on the smooth surfaces. Somehow it makes me all the more wary and I steer clear, both of us getting as close as we dare to that part-open door.

As I do so I realise there's a problem with my comms

system, some sort of faint static. I look over at Kall and he's noticed it too. He's tapping on the side of his helmet, thinking it's a speaker error. My heart leaps though – it's Sim, trying to contact me! With the bay doors half-open I must be able to receive some scrap of a signal.

Before I can do anything I find myself flooded with light, I look around in confusion, thinking the ship's power has returned, before I realise it's the drone.

–purging sys—

I don't catch the rest of its message as there's a dull pop in my ear. The comms failsafe has clicked it dead. There's no time to worry about that though. The drone's lights shudder as whatever system purge goes through then it lurches forward and slams into me.

7

Light streaks across my eyes as I'm thrown back. The impact jolts me from my surroundings, the universe contracting around me. Everything is movement and smears of light. Confusion and panic and pain. I twist sideways as the drone barges into me and on past. It half-rebounds, still accelerating but spinning as it does so.

I feel a crunch and snap reverberate through my body as I fall back. One boot dislodges and my foot flails as I pinwheel in zero-g. It affords me a view of the drone as it surges on and hits Kall. I feel pain in my chest, dull and remote but enough to panic me as I watch Kall take a similar blow. Without my armour he's snapped back, boots locked on the floor as his body hinges at the knee.

I hear nothing. The comms link has failed and I've only the heave of my breath, the shriek of warning tones in my suit. Still I see his agony. A convulsion of pain runs through his body as he slams back against the floor behind him. Sparks burst from the smashed control unit on his chest.

Anchored by one boot only I swing around, following

the drone's progress as it rebounds again. It moves drunkenly, lights spinning toward the partially open door. In my dazed state I feel confused at that, the drone racing towards freedom. The voice at the back of my head – the idiot that was frightened of ghosts – now wonders why it couldn't wait. Couldn't take care for those last few metres and had to rush instead like a panic-stricken animal.

Then the drone strikes the edge of the bay-door and I feel the shudder through my feet. That gets me thinking sensibly again. I watch aghast as the drone scrapes and jolts against the metal edge. Without atmosphere there is just a brief flickering of sparks as it pushes jerkily into the space between the doors. There's enough room for it to get through but the surge of acceleration has brought it hard against the side and it's ended up twisted in the gap.

The drone's mini-thrusters fire erratically. For a moment I don't understand what it's doing but then it hits me. The thing's not trying to get outside, it's trying to turn. It doesn't care about leaving this ghost-wreck, it's coming back to finish the job!

I try to run to Kall, but as soon as I get my boot down it locks into place. I heave at my feet and eventually they release me. One after the other, my boots do as I ask and I stagger a few steps, still disorientated. Kall hasn't moved, he's flopped back, loose and limp. A firefly spark whips across my face, distracting me further. I recoil from the movement as a second comes, this one slamming into the back of my helmet. Not hard, just a rattle and scrape on my armour, but it slows me further.

The drone is still moving strangely, like it has a novice pilot or the impact with the door has damaged it. Either way, I feel like I'm moving in a dream – slow and ponderous. The distance between myself and Kall suddenly seems huge. A gulf I can't hope to cross. The firefly crashes into my helmet again and this time I realise it's one of my mini drones, battering with all the blind purpose of a maybug. I swipe it away but it comes straight back so I grab it and slam it hard on the floor.

A faint scrape alerts me to the other one. Its moving awkwardly, almost crawling on my shoulder. The sensation is repulsive – all the more horrifying when I realise it's trying to dock again, worm its way into the suit like a tick. I smash that too and toss the remains across the bay.

Able to focus on the drone again, I realise its comms array is broken. It hangs loose, swinging around as the drone manages to free itself of the door. That's what I felt snap when it rammed me. A flush of relief surges through my body, but then something else too – shock realisation catching up at last.

Blunt though the array is, it's still a metal protrusion out the front of the drone. Hardly a spear I know, but the drone rammed it into my chest deliberately. A less heavy-duty suit might easily have been breached. As it is, I look down, searching for damage, but it appears cosmetic. The drone came off worse in the attack but still, it attacked me. If it'd not broken on me, the array would have punched right into Kall's ribcage.

And it's coming back for another charge.

I'm still moving slowly, limbs shaky. Eventually the shock recedes and my brain recognises I need to act. It's getting ready to hit me again unless I do something. I get the image of the knights of ancient times in their armour, tilting on a jousting ground. I can't outrun it, not a chance. Kall still isn't even moving. But I've got a lance too.

I raise my arm and flip up the firing panel, almost hitting the button in my haste. At point-blank range there's little aiming to be done, but little time to do it in either. I press the button even as I give the verbal command to fire the harpoon. My arm judders as the coil-gun mechanism kicks it forward and a manoeuvring jet on my shoulder compensates.

I can barely see with the drone's lights full in my face, but the harpoon slams into metal somewhere between those and the whole thing jolts back.

The force drives it through the opening between the doors, a thin cable stretching out between us. One light winks out, broken against the left-hand door. The other spins wildly, a shining sword slashing at the black. The harpoon's driven deep into the body of the drone. Sim hadn't added atmosphere shielding or anything so it's not even as tough as my EVA suit. The damage must be immense and I feel a flash of fear that it'll explode, but it's still going backwards with thrusters spurting erratically.

I release the cable and watch that spring forward, the slack drifting up like sea-string on an ocean current. Then it whips away, the drone wheeling further and further into space. Not waiting to watch, I lumber over to Kall. As I grasp his arm, I feel a response and almost weep with relief. My training is in charge of my body however and while I'm calling uselessly to him, I start to inspect his suit.

There are no tears, but the control unit on the front is smashed. Even if my comms hadn't gone down, his is a wreck. Pulling myself forward, I look Kall full in the face and see blessed signs of life. His face is contorted with pain, he's mouthing something too, but he's awake somehow. I can't tell what damage there is, but the drone failed to get him straight on. Maybe a childhood of contact sport saved his life even as it wrecked his original knee.

'Remote sensors,' I yell at my suit, hardly able to remember how the secondary functions work.

–comms link inoperable– the suit replies with its usual dispassion.

'Alternative methods?'

–invalid command–

I try not to scream in frustration. The suit is several orders stupider than the ship's computer and I need my brain to be working better than this.

'List alternative remote diagnostics and suit-to-suit links,' I hazard.

–secondary communications–no response in vicinity–burst transmission– Here a stuttering series of rapid flashes erupts from a pinprick circle on my chest *–no response in vicinity–manual link–not engaged–*

'Manual link? What? Where? Locate.'

–central digit on gauntlet–

I look, hardly believing it and having never heard of such a thing before, but there it is – a black circle on the pad of each gauntlet's middle finger. I quickly search Kall's suit for a corresponding contact point – nothing on his hands but there's a black oval below the rim of the helmet that I'd always thought was just decoration.

'Read the damn user manual, Song!' I hiss at myself as I press finger to pad and wait an eternity.

–manual link established– the suit reports before it's replaced with the sound of Kall in pain.

'Kall! Can you hear me?' I yell.

'Song? Howling dark,' he moans.

'Suit, run diagnostic.'

–sensors non-functional–air reserve stable–life signs absent–

'What?' I yell before I realise. I can see Kall's bloody

alive, it's just the suit doesn't have the capacity to tell one way or another.

'Hurts,' Kall whispers to me. 'Song...'

In the next moment I see his eyes roll up. His body goes limp in my hands and I howl with terror and frustration. He might be dead, he might just be unconscious, but there's nothing I can do out in this vacuum. Clearly there's some internal damage, but with his sensors offline I can't find out where the problem is. Even with a manual link meaning my suit can run his, there's little enough working in there for it to use.

I have to get him out. Turning to the part-open bay door, I gauge the space. There's easily enough room for both of us and yet...

Can we trust it? I wonder. *Do I even have a choice?*

Reaching down, I manually disengage Kall's boots. Being freed from the tether brings no sort of reaction from him. The big man's a dead weight and fear judders inside me as I hope he's not already dead. Still I hesitate. I bring him closer to the door and look out. There's no movement, no light on that outer section of the wreck. No systems running that I can see, but I didn't see anything earlier when the other one shut on us.

From outside there's a rogue flash of light that I realise is the drone – still spinning, still trying to compensate for the harpoon bolt driven into its guts. I flinch at the sight though it's a fair way off already. It doesn't look like it's coming back soon, that's one positive.

With a good grip on Kall, I edge towards the opening. Do I push him through first – use him ghoulishly as a test to spring the trap? Without me he's dead either way, but it seems insane that I'm having the debate with myself at all. He's floating horizontally so while I try to work out what the sensible course of action is, I stand him upright. He's still limp and without gravity it doesn't make much difference either way, but no point spending longer in danger than necessary as we go through.

There's no blood inside his helmet, not that I can see anyway. I take that as a good sign and manoeuvre him around so we can go together in one swift burst. I hesitate though and, anchored by me, momentum swings Kall's arm up into the gap.

That moment saves me. That stupid fear of ghosts I never knew I had until I got stuck out in this wreck; it keeps me alive as the undamaged door whips across my face. It crashes into the other side with enough force to crack my suit like an egg. Kall's unarmoured arm doesn't even put up a fight. I find myself screaming with terror as he jolts in my hands – nothing dramatic. Little more than a twitch, but then his hand is gone.

The whole shuttle bay judders with the impact and I howl as I lurch backwards – unheard by anything or anyone – dragging Kall with me. Blood sprays out, garnet globules staining the white sweep of lights. If there had been gravity I'd have fallen on my backside and sobbed but as it is, the boots keep me tethered and the rest of me flops uselessly. I don't have the manual contact engaged but I see enough of a reaction from Kall all the same. His muscles twitch and haul at me. I can't see his face well. It might be I only imagine his eyes wide with pain and horror, but it burns into my brain all the same. The squirt of blood continues, floating weightlessly across the bay. I grab at his injured arm and miss, managing to bat it away and worsen the escape of blood.

On my second attempt, I grab it while shrieking commands at my suit. It has a general-purpose sealant built in, not intended for medical emergencies but good enough to patch a suit tear. At this point it doesn't matter, however. Even as I'm pulling the short nozzle out from a narrow slot on my arm, I realise the flow of blood has slowed. The suit has contracted around Kall's body as air is sucked out. I patch the hole where his hand and half his forearm used to be, then seek out the manual interface again.

It takes me a short while, but my suit stabilises the air pressure again. By that point however there's a bloody mess inside his helmet. I can see a thin trickle emerging like a parasitic worm from Kall's mouth and nose, much more drifting up from the direction of his injured arm. I uselessly shout commands at my suit, but it can't do anything to help him. My words devolve into a wordless babble, but I refuse to give up.

Compressions on his heart, I think to myself. It's all I've got left. A difficult thing in zero-g anyway, but if the suit can't do anything else, I've got to try. I manoeuvre him down to the floor so there's a surface behind him and place my gauntlet on his chest.

It's then that I feel it. The give of his ribcage. I don't push down hard, I'm still feeling my way into position with the massive power-assisted gloves. All the same, his chest is just wrecked. The right-hand side of the ribcage is noticeably depressed compared to the left. Even a small amount of pressure drives more blood up towards his face. More than I can expect anyone to survive, even someone of Kall's size and strength.

I release him and just stare down at Kall. There's no movement, no recognition in those eyes. They're open but see nothing, looking sightlessly up past my head. I shudder and once I start I can't stop for a while. An animal whimper escapes my lips and I feel my hands tremble uncontrollably, a chill deep in my bones. Weeping in an EVA suit is a bad idea though and the sight of a few drops flying free in front of my face is enough to shake me out of it.

I push upright and retreat from Kall's body. Suddenly I can't bear to be near it and there's blood still flying free in the bay. As I do so there's the stutter of greenish light on a blank wall panel – just a brief impression of movement before fading away again. The fight/flight instinct kicks in and I retreat further. Somehow I feel the gloating presence of some enraged and senselessly mad spirit. I lurch around, looking for other threats but the shuttle bay is still again. Even the blood has stopped, hanging like frozen rubies in the half-light. Everything else in there is long dead, the lights gone as though they'd never been there. Except not quite. It's not some ghost stalking me through darkened corridors, I know that much, but there's something here. Some scrap of power remains in this dead ship. Either it means I'm not as alone as I'd like or the residual systems are so hopelessly degraded everything is a threat to me.

Part of me wants to weep, part of me screams to get moving. The part that wants to run away wins. I look over at the bay door. It's still closed. The damage means it's not a perfect fit, but I'm not shifting those huge lumps of metal. All the same I try my expander – it's literally made for that sort of thing. I should have tried it to brace the gap before heading out but in my panic didn't think of it. And now Kall's dead as a result.

Trying not to snivel and waste time cursing myself, I detach the expander and fit the claws in the gap between doors. It's a long shot, but it's a powerful little unit and I'm eager for a task to focus on to calm myself down.

Once I hook it up to my suit's power pack it quickly engages and starts to try to drive the doors apart. Even at full power however, it can't shift them. Rather than burn it out I stop, packing it away again. I need to find another way out. It's looks rather like the wreck has other ideas, however.

'And that's the problem,' I say to nothing and no one. 'Those doors shut on me, they weren't randomly firing.'

The static. The drone's last transmission.

'It purged its data and my comms link dropped,' I force myself to say out loud, accepting it as reality. 'That's no malfunction. That's a failsafe.'

Chill fingers of fear run down my spine as I put two and two together. The scraps of power left in this wreck are being used. Those flickers of light aren't incidental either, but some sort of system powering up what it needed to control door mechanisms, even hack the drone.

Our suit comms and main systems are separate for exactly that reason, but the drone is built for remote control. When something tried to worm into us, my comms overloaded and fell dark, Kall's too. The drone had no such defence and could only purge its main data. It wiped itself and the clone of the *Sakakawea*'s computer stored there to preserve information security, abandoning the drone's shell as unimportant.

Which normally it would be. Every ship has them after all. Stealing one isn't worth the effort of what's required to crack the core shell inside. Unless information isn't of interest. If you just want to kill an interloper, a metre-long lump of metal and engines might well prove useful. I look at Kall again, but can't bear the sight of him any longer. Shame wells up inside me, shame and disgust. I was his captain. I was the one who should have kept him safe. Instead, mere minutes after leading him in here, he was dead.

I can't bring myself to even speak – to apologise to his corpse or say some trite rubbish in his memory. My throat is too tight, a fist of guilt lodged firmly in my gullet. Instead I just turn away, uselessly rubbing at the spots of his blood on my gauntlets. I'm not as careful getting out of the shuttle bay. I'm too frightened and shocked to care. All I want is to be out of there fast and if some door slams on me as I do so, it'll be the least I deserve. Outside I do stop though. The hangar beyond feels colder as well as darker without the drone's lights. For a moment I turn back towards where I've left the shuttle, but I realise that could be stupid. There's a remote piloting facility after all, which means it's open to comms manipulation too.

Still I want to risk it. If nothing else, I want to talk to the AI there just to hear it talk back to me. But I know that's insane. To do so would require a reboot of my comms or a hardwire and neither is a great idea right now. The shuttle itself is a more dangerous prospect than the drone, far larger and able to crush me against the wall with ease. I feel my fingers twitching, like I'm trying to play piano in this freezing vacuum of death.

'Right – think, Song. You can't help Kall now so think about your kids instead. Think about getting home to them. Think about seeing their faces again and promising never to go into the great dark again. Focus dammit. There's no way back, so what do you do?'

To my right there's a broken craft of some kind. It's wedged pretty tightly between some sort of lifting arm and an array of metal contraptions I can't work out the use of. Most importantly it's all broken and there's a space below it. I head over there with my heart in my mouth, but nothing jumps out at me and the hangar lights stay dark. Inside a minute, I've fitted myself beneath it, awkwardly but there's enough space to be sure I'm not going to get stuck. The space resembles a child's tent of blankets. As stupid as it seems, it's that security I want – need.

I settle myself down, out of sight from most of the hangar and my heart begins to calm. False security I know, on one level at least, but I'm jumping at ghosts. Before I deal with the main problem of eventual asphyxiation, I'm going to hide under a blanket where the monsters can't get me.

'I need to get out,' I tell myself once my heart and mind have reached a steady purr. 'Outside the hull where the *Sak* has a chance of finding me. That bit I'll work on later, getting out is the only important thing right now. How do I do it?'

I bring up what maps I've got. There's a partial of the exterior stored on my suit, part of the packet the drone transferred. I almost weep with relief at the sight of it. It's nothing detailed but gives me an idea of where I should be heading. Without that I'd stand little chance of navigating an alien ship of this size before my air ran out.

The damaged fighter bays lie below us from where I'm viewing it, but I don't know if I want to go that way. In the opposite direction there are the large breaches in the hull. It's a longer journey though, maybe twice as far – assuming there's a clear path at all.

'If those are fighter bays, there's weaponry and who knows what else that could be co-opted into killing me.'

I speak for my own benefit, both the grown-up and the child in this conversation. At least one of those needs a whole lot of reassurance.

'Still – it's the obvious escape route. Too obvious? Does that matter? Think, Song!'

It's a struggle, reasoning this out while I can't stop thinking of my family, and Kall's bloodied face looming at the back of my mind like a spirit seeking justice. And that's before I try to second-guess some alien system that's likely so corrupted and malfunctioning it can't work the way it's supposed to. Even if I knew what it was made to do.

'How did it find me? Spotted the shuttle or something else? If it's got internal scanners, it hardly matters where I go. This ghost will find me no matter what.'

Unbidden, the image of a shade drifting down corridors appears in my mind, searching hungrily for someone to blame for its death. I shake my head and curse myself out for indulging my fears. I have to get a grip.

'Shuttle it is. I have to assume it's still looking but hasn't found me yet. The lights must be a guide – tell me where it's searching. Maybe. Probably. Probably not, come to think of it, but I can't stay here forever. It's as good an idea as any so it's a risk I'll have to take.'

I consult the outside scan again. It looks a short distance to the ruined section until you appreciate the scale. Then it looks like madness except for the fact that's a big open section and I want to get outside. If there's a path anywhere, it'll be there. There's simply too much space to have it all blocked, on top of the fact it'll be easier to find.

Navigation inside this alien wreck will be hellish even without jumping at shadows. From the image I have, I'm guessing there's a good kilometre of ripped-open hull there. More than enough for one frightened little girl to wriggle outside, hopefully nothing even close to functioning doors that could slam shut on me.

'Frightened little girl with a gods-damned harpoon!' I remind myself feebly. 'Give me a harpoon and a plan and I'll conquer the world. Or kill a whale, or something like that.'

I shake my head. 'Shut up, Song. Get moving instead.'

I work my way out of the den and check around. It's given me a moment to think, a chance to establish what I'm doing, but right now I need to go. If this ghost has got anything it can move around the wreck, I want to be well clear of this place when that happens. Before I do anything else however, I investigate my suit's functions and feel a tiny boost when I find what I'm looking for.

'Next time, Jamal, I promise I'll read the manual more carefully,' I mutter.

The suits aren't only designed for space but hostile surfaces as well. Surfaces where there might be indigenous lifeforms. As a result, it's got a built in motion-tracker. Nothing military-grade of course, but decent as an afterthought from the designers. The range is a hundred metres in open ground, just enough to warn you if you're being stalked. Less in here of course, but any movement at all is a sign I'm in trouble. I switch it on to run in the background. The drain on my suit isn't significant. I'll asphyxiate long before I run out of power.

In the middle of the hangar I pause and try to remember where I saw lights flickering. There are a number of exits in addition to what is some sort of cargo platform. There's a gap beside that, top and bottom, but no ladder, just the now-ubiquitous hand-holds. I head to the centre of the hangar and survey my options. It's then that I spot the debris blocking one of the exits – or rather, blocking the doors from shutting. It's no obstacle to someone in zero-g.

'Is that suspicious, or was someone else trying not to get killed by doors?'

My question brings no answers, but if I don't get lucky, I'm going to be dead soon anyway. I go through.

8

I emerge into what appears to be an enormous service tunnel. My little lights don't show me much, but the impression of size looms in the spaces they cannot penetrate. It must run for hundreds of metres both left and right and is taller than the hangar behind me. I can only make out the barest detail of the ceiling, forty metres above. Without the drone's scanning abilities, I'm having to guess at all too much, but I'm less worried about exploration now.

The main feature is a pair of rails that protrude from halfway up the walls, each one a metre thick. They run all the way down the tunnel from what I can see. Everything is functional; there's little of the artistry I guessed at from the outside on show.

The rails suggest some sort of transport system, perhaps carriages able to run well above the heads of those walking or even mid-size ships. The *Sakakawea* would certainly fit. A ship this big would need multiple large conduits. I'm glad of my EVA suit giving me a sense of orientation. Otherwise the sense of falling would be terrifying as I look down that yawning shaft. It's largely clear to my left, just a few tangled heaps twenty-odd metres away.

I decide not to investigate, scientific curiosity be damned. We can do that bit on the next trip. Off to the right there's more debris. One great smashed lump that could once have been a cargo transport, damaged machinery and a trio of large spheres connected by rods that hang above it all. That looks incongruous to me, smooth grey sides that are blank but for long trails of... jagged tears? Claw marks? Whatever caused them, I want to avoid anything capable of inflicting that.

Dotted around the walls and floor are plenty of smaller, amorphous heaps. I can only guess at what those are or were, but I steer clear for practical reasons. If they were bodies of the former occupants, it's likely there'll be little more than dust and fragments left. Nothing to be learned from the remains and a lot that could clog joints and obscure my vision.

As I start to cross the tunnel, heading for an open section that looks promising, I see a distant flutter of light. It's not enough to see by but it gives me a jolt all the same. I freeze, a few metres from any sort of cover. Just as I'm debating what to do a light comes on, far enough that I can't gauge the distance, but not just some elusive flickering. This is a steady shine with a faintly green tint. There's nothing moving near it, not that I can see anyway, but it remains steady while I tremble.

Terror clamps tight around my throat. Just when my lungs start to object, the light vanishes as unexpectedly as it appeared. As it does so, something closer to hand illuminates – near the top of the massive service tunnel. There's a long bank of windows there, mere shapes amid the darkness until a glow appears from somewhere within. I fight to take a breath then try to focus on what I can see. I glimpse red on a wall panel and something blue in the centre of the room, turning slowly. Perhaps a projection schematic? I can only see one end as it drifts around but it could well be an image of the wreck.

The movement remains steady for a short while before vanishing again, returning the tunnel to darkness. My anxiety only increases though. It's all so deliberate and calculated I can't help but wonder what the purpose is. At least this time it doesn't appear to be directed at me. That I'm a witness seems almost irrelevant. Perhaps it is all just the random firing of a decrepit system. The nearer one wasn't particularly close and even if it had been right above me, I'd hardly have been illuminated more than I am already. I'm half-cringing at the prospect of suddenly being bathed in light, but nothing happens and the tunnel returns to darkness.

I remain paralysed by indecision for half a minute. Kall's bloodied face swims before my eyes and I almost turn back, expecting to see his corpse floating behind me. Tethered by guilt, by condemnation that I'm leaving him here in this tomb. He'd hate that, I know, and it makes me want to weep, but I can't lug his body along. I nod, as though reassuring myself it's the right decision. Of course it is. Anything that hampers me getting back to my family has to be left behind. My wreck-diving instructors hammered that point home hard – *"survive first, feel guilty if you want afterwards but make sure you survive to do so."*

Just as I'm getting myself together I see a pale flash way off to my left. I whimper and turn but it's faint. I only get a glimpse, a sense of shape before it's gone, but it does my nerves no good at all. It looked like a figure in movement, limbs and legs silently working before vanishing again.

I tell myself the motion tracker is silent, yell it inside my helmet as panic sloshes through my mind and threatens to drown my thoughts. It was nothing physical, that much I know. Hardly reassuring to someone jumping at ghosts, but even here I know that's foolishness. A malfunctioning light, a power surge in something that was ancient before humanity ever reached the stars. My spooked brain provided the rest, that's all.

Still the fear of being out in the open grips me. I disengage my boots, using a kick and a jolt from my suit jets to propel me across the space. I glide through to the wide gap on the far side and on into a crossroads space of pillars with exits on all sides. I manage to arrest my progress before I fly across the entire space, catching a long metal bar with one hand. That proves strong enough to stop me then I push down, sending myself back towards the floor where my boots engage once more.

This section looks different, less clinical than the hangars and service tunnel. It's clearly a functional space given the ten or twelve different doorways, some closed up, others open and black, but the edges are smoother. There's a hint of colour even after all this time. Faded greens and blues marking the walls and ceiling mainly, but nothing I'd describe as writing still.

There's more debris, scattered heaps and solid, angular objects in addition to damage to one doorway. Mostly the signs of violence are heat warping and long shallow gouges in walls. In the centre of the crossroads there's a column composed of multiple tubes, at least six. They alternate between large, looking capable of carrying twenty humans depending on how snug they're willing to stand, and smaller two-person tubes. Given the oval doors on each, I'm guessing they're a type of elevator.

I cast my lights around and see more hand-holds on the walls. On the tubes and the ceiling too. It makes me wonder whether the builders of this craft were incredibly agile. The layout continues to suggest artificial gravity fields, but there are openings well above head-height. Now that I inspect the ceiling properly I see it's marked with regular bubble-like shapes. Open at one end and about four metres across, they could certainly be reached only by skilled human climbers.

Continuing my sweep, I see another access tube. This one is behind me and open. It abuts the service tunnel entrance and appears to contain no ladder, just a regular array of the familiar hand-holds. What really catches my attention is the symbol cut into the metal above the opening; three ovals just like we saw by the light outside. Open, part-open and closed. It's obviously not part of the original decoration. Some sharp tool has been used but it's a skilful rendering.

'Come into my parlour,' I mutter to myself.

It leaves me in a quandary. I'm trapped here because I followed this symbol. A deliberate invitation before something tried to kill me, hastily and chaotically. I look again at the tube. With the hand-holds jutting out, it's unlikely to have any sort of mechanism moving down it. I know I'm second-guessing an alien species, but I can't see any reason why it wouldn't be either smooth or with a rail to follow. And if I'm right that this is a species that climbs better than humans, a manual shaft could easily look like this.

Only when I remember this whole ship is basically a tomb do I step towards the tube. I want to go up and this appears to be the best available option. Any invitation was left for some being long-dead. If there's a degraded security protocol trying to kill me, the tube is reassuringly free of mechanisms.

I take a closer look and it does appear to be what I expect. The tube is clear upon inspection, both up and down. It requires slightly comical manoeuvring to get my head so the lights are looking straight up, but eventually I manage it and the hand-holds go on for as far as I can make out. How far it goes is anyone's guess, but beyond the range of my lamps there's a tiny point of light. Maybe a hundred metres up. I can't make out more detail, but it's steady – perhaps an exit to the tube with some sort of light beyond.

Belatedly I discover there is a door, flush against the curved inner surface and hard to spot at first. When I do see it I flinch back, but it does nothing – fails to murder me in any way. Eventually I look closer and see a tangle of dark cables hanging down from its lower surface. They glitter in the light of my suit lamps, unlike any wiring I've ever seen, crumbling to dust when I touch them with my boot. Some of it sticks, coats my toe the way there's blood residue frozen to my fingers. All the same, seeing something has been damaged on the door leaves me oddly reassured.

There's no handle but I shove then pull the door as hard as I dare and it doesn't move a millimetre. Hardly a scientific test, but that's all I've got. If this door has been broken or tampered with, there's less chance it'll kill or trap me. I disengage my boots and manoeuvre inside, floating gently with one hand to steady me. Still nothing happens so I start pulling myself upwards.

I go slowly. As solid as my suit is, I'm not going to test it by zooming along and catching a stray hand-hold. Despite the fact it'll get tiring over time, I go hand over hand and pull myself up. The repetition is a welcome thing to focus on. It's strange and uncomfortable still. There are handholds on three sides so I just use one set and keep my bulky suit clear of the others.

As I travel I'm more aware than ever how claustrophobic it is inside an EVA suit. With this tube less than two metres across I'm visually enclosed and left to hope I'm not ignoring hazards. I check above me every ten handholds or so, but the tube remains empty and the dull glow is steady as I plod towards it.

After a few minutes, I'm there – or rather, floating just below it, nervous to pop my head up. I find myself listening for clues but of course there's nothing to hear, not out in a vacuum, and all I have to go on is the light. It's faint, just noticeable against the complete blackness everywhere else, but with a discernible green tint. The light it casts is regular and from the edge of shadow around the inside of the tube, it seems to be coming from something well away from the tube itself.

Coming up from underneath, I see the door's been messed with in the same way as down below. More of those glittering, organic-looking cables hang loose and a small slot among several tight-fitting pieces suggests a component has been removed. Eventually I summon up the courage to continue and bring myself up level with the opening.

I discover a huge domed chamber, dominated by an elegant sculpture of some sort of tree. The tree itself is the source of the faint light, made of some pale stone that emits a greenish glow no brighter than hazy moonlight. It's huge as sculptures go – I guess a good thirty metres high – with three broad, gracefully curved trunks that merge just above head-height. It's beautiful too, a smoothly organic surface with every line and edge highlighted by that inner radiance.

A religious function perhaps? I wonder if this species took its gods into space in a way humans neglected to. Certainly too big for simple artistry. Even on a ship this size, space would be at a premium, but it seems unlikely to be purely functional either. I'm filled with a sudden yearning to fetch Kall's body – to lay him to rest somewhere like this. The calm glow, the soothing sense of reverence. This is where he should be left if anywhere, but the idea of back-tracking is foolish, I know.

Its many branches fill most of the room's space. Each one supports six nest-like bowls of varying size, the smallest easily big enough for a human.

Beyond the great tree there's little to see. Doorways lead off the chamber on all sides, hand-holds mark the wall. As I look closer I realise there are more on the tree itself. There's a mess on the floor too, misshapen lumps, dust, and hard-frozen liquid, but little else. It's so devoid of objects the temple idea remains plausible. The hand-holds suggest movement all over the tree which rather spoils the image, but who's to guess there?

Wary of any light even if this steady glow is a world away from the threatening stutters elsewhere, I continue up the tube to see where it leads. Unfortunately just five metres up I discover a problem. There's an obstacle blocking my path, an X shape that appears to have been crudely welded to the sides. I don't know if I can make it through the gaps, but I know it would be tight. For a moment I try to work out an angle to approach but an EVA suit is bulky.

The powerpack is modest, but even with the best scrubbers around there still needs to be a quantity of air involved and that takes up space. I could probably cut the bars but it'll take time and power, plus leave sharp edges. While I'm deciding however, I notice more oval images, engraved in the tube's metal interior, just above the doorway.

'It seems someone wants me out this way,' I mutter. 'Given the alternative, I think I'll be polite and do as I'm asked.'

I take a deep breath and leave the tube.

9

I walk slowly, unable to shake the feeling I've invaded hallowed ground. Needlessly cautious of echoes in the vacuum, imagining sounds in this silence. The faint glow of the tree only gives a general sense of space and proportion, but that's enough. It stops me flinching at the great slabs of shadow that reach in whenever I turn. After a few steps I realise I'm being foolish and disengage my boots, pushing off to the nearest of the nests. There's detritus in the bottom, small blocks of metal caked in dust and dirt.

From the nest I've got a better view and see there's a gallery of sorts on my left. Partitioned by glass that's been cracked and shot-through in places, it contains a jumble of objects I take to be furniture. One corner has large units of panels and alcoves, everything smooth and round-edged except where they've been smashed.

Beyond it there's a light. For a moment I don't realise, thinking it's a reflection of the tree's glow, but then the shape nags at me and I realise this has no green tint. There's something past this gallery, a corridor and adjoining rooms. One of those has light shining out through open windows and doors. It's as weak as that of the tree but colder, faintly tinted blue. It's the shape that catches my attention, oval windows framing the light.

I look closer but I can't see where the light is coming from. It seems to fill the room but no more. With a small push I drift across to the great window overlooking the tree and grab a hand-hold on one of the mullions to anchor myself. From there I've got a slightly better view, but it doesn't help a whole lot. There is something in the room, a number of things in fact but I can't make out much detail. Debris hangs in the air, jagged edges and straight lines are all I can make out. It's a frozen tableau, like the still of an explosion but...

I freeze. There's something else in there. Sharp black edges jut outwards like the explosion itself. The wall obscures my view and shifting position does little to help at that angle, but there's something in the centre of the room, dark against the light. I can't tell where the source of the light is, but it doesn't seem to touch this the way it does the rest.

My own lights have a similar lack of effect on it, as though I'm looking at nothing real. I can make out a design on the wall, complex interlinked circles, and rectangular lines above that suggest storage lockers. Everything is faintly illuminated except the angular central object which is so dark it seems to have no form, no dimensions.

From the top of the window I can't see much, just the tangle of awkward shapes like thick branches laden with blades reaching up from the floor. It doesn't look synthetic to me, but the dark outline hardly seems organic either. Anyways, surely any sort of foliage would have long disintegrated by now?

As I watch the light unexpectedly blinks out. I recoil in shock, my helmet lights jerking across the room. They cut long shadows as I drift backwards and I glimpse a sudden flash of movement. Objects that were hanging motionless spin crazily, the inky branches lash in a silent display of fury.

A second later and the light appears again. It illuminates a different view of chaos and I blink in shock. For a second everything still seems to be in movement, slowing rapidly to a stop as though swimming in viscous gel before inertia takes hold. I continue moving away from the glass, fast enough that I need to turn and catch myself before I strike the nest behind. Before I do so I see more movement though, a thin metallic shape no larger than a standard comm-pad.

It pulls free of the blue light and flies gently forward, moving as any normal object would in zero-g, despite everything behind it already back to motionless. I watch in fascination and horror as it spins towards me and bangs against the glass near where I'd been floating.

The glass doesn't shatter, it's not even marked by the impact but still I flinch. Rebounding, the object slows to a halt in the normal fashion rather than oddly sluggish and frozen. What's going on in that room I can't even guess right now. All I want is to get away from that glimpsed tangle of horror. Somehow it's caught in the light, pinned there. The stirrings of an idea tickle the back of my mind, but my body is too busy to listen.

I turn and push off, heading towards one exit. There are multiple doorways here. It's clearly a hub of some sort, but the largest has a pair of blast doors halfway closed. As I get closer my lights pierce the darkness to reveal a largely empty hallway beyond. No jagged, unnatural shapes that don't catch the light. No dangerous obstacles. No carved symbols either, not on any of the exits, but a main thoroughfare is probably my best bet for finding a path out.

The blast doors look damaged, not jammed open but melted at the top. Whatever alloy comprises this ship, it's tough, but some weapon seems to have had its measure. The doors slide along a runner as wide as my thigh, but have fused into it so completely it's impossible to tell where one ends and the other begins. For my purposes it's encouraging, but I doubt the ship's crew felt the same.

Before I slip through the gap between doors I glance back, up at the gallery where I can see the blueish lambent light trace the lines of the glass. Nothing seems to have changed, but I'm glad to leave it behind all the same. I'm such a jumble of nerves I don't want to leave the tree's slight brightness, but the glimpse of movement has left me shaken. I press on into the dark with barely a moment's hesitation.

Beyond the hallway is a small, empty room. It feels more like an airlock than anything more and leads me to a broad corridor, three times as high as it is wide. Again there are handholds up most of the walls, a variety of alcoves and rooms set seemingly at random heights. I clamber up to one to take a look inside but there's little there. Returning to the nominal floor I end up walking for a short while, trying to imagine what sort of creatures this was designed for.

Mostly I fail. I'm looking for inky tentacles in every shadow instead, fingers twitching towards the harpoon at each imagined threat. None comes. No lights flicker, nothing at all moves. Here the wreck feels more like a mausoleum than before – empty slots for coffins on either side. Only my passing disturbs the dust of millennia and, looking back out of paranoia as I regularly do, even that returns to heavy stillness before I've gone far.

Pipes or bridges cross my path as I walk. There are regular protrusions from the ceiling, hoops through which something has been looped. Most of that something has disintegrated long ago bar some sort of fastenings that look like ceramic. Again, I decide not to investigate. They're surrounded by a haze of dust, the remains of something organic that collapsed in on itself after a few thousand years.

Instead I walk until my path ends, abruptly. It's a small shaft where three such "alleyways" have converged. I'd been walking the lowest of them so I push up to the others and direct my lights down each. There's little enough to see. More pipes and narrow bridges on the first, many steeply sloped, but that's it. The other shaft is even less exciting. No lights to interrupt the darkness. I pause to consult my map, laughable as it is to use the term for something so rudimentary. Without the drone's sensors I can't flesh out any of the detail, only use the suit's basic functions to estimate my location. It won't be perfect, but hopefully it'll suffice.

Before I guess at a direction, I do a careful check around. If there was something trying to guide my route, I'd need a hint here, but there's nothing – no ovals or helpful arrows. All I have is a choice between the two, but the higher path seems sensible. It's still a diversion from the direction I think I should be going in, but hopefully closer and... well, up is good right?

That's what I tell myself as I continue on, ignoring the fact I'm in zero-g. Up is good. I'm getting nearer. I'm going to get out of here. I'm going to find a way out to the *Sakakawea* and home to my family. I'm going to...

The litany is cut short when there's an eruption of blue-tinted light up ahead on my left – a few metres ahead and almost blinding after the pitch black. I stumble sideways and let slip a tiny not-very-captainly shriek. Then I look inside the newly-lit room.

10

It's empty.

After that pants-wetting flash of light, there's nothing to be afraid of. Other than the fact the bastard thing just flicked on as I was passing, of course. Coincidence? I don't bloody think so.

The urge to shoot something doesn't so much well up as explode inside me. I want to yell and curse every being that ever once walked this wreck, throw objects and smash what's left of the place. But when no one can hear you scream and there's basically nothing at hand to break, it feels a bit pointless. I do none of it beyond a few feeble words even my children probably know. Part of me is numb after Kall's death, the rest of me too focused on keeping myself in check.

For a moment I don't do anything, other than the panting for breath that is. Then I cast my lights around and notice something I'd been about to walk past. One of the many recesses leads to a side passage – small and cramped but able to admit my EVA suit. Is this really some sort of message? If there's something watching me, I've no idea how it's doing it.

The ghost theory is starting to sound a little more plausible at this point. If it wasn't for the fact I've seen how *that* vid ends, I'd have discounted it entirely. I know perfectly well that science disproved ghosts long ago. Out here in the great dark though, I've no intention of tempting fate even if I'm not adopting it as a working hypothesis.

The side passage should really be dank and gloomy. Instead it's just narrow and devoid of anything interesting. Even on a ship this large, I'd expect to find more. Part of me thinks a salvage team will discover this species tidies like my husband. Uncluttered rooms and corridors, with every concealed locker stuffed with junk.

Before I decide anything I inspect the lit-up room. There's a variety of studs embedded in the ceiling, a groove around the upper section of the wall. A bench has been drawn out of one side wall, other panels suggesting there's more furnishings that could be revealed. Beyond that though the room is empty. I've already passed dozens like it. Most don't lead anywhere, they're just large single spaces that seem neither storerooms nor offices.

Two apertures on my near side plus the door – all open, covering panels neatly withdrawn into the structure of the wall. Even before I get right up to it, there's clearly nothing terrifying inside. Still, I'm not going in. Just to add to the creepiness of this, the light seems to have no source that I can discern. Instead I scout around and eventually find a piece of debris. It's a scrap of metal, smooth-edged with a ragged side where something less durable had been attached.

Keeping a few metres short of the doorway I toss it forward. It glides with the usual smoothness of zero-g then reaches the light and inexplicably slows, coming to a halt maybe ten centimetres past the threshold. There it hangs, not moving in any way. Even the slight spin fades to nothing almost immediately, as though the room is full of something much denser than air.

Puzzled, I hunt for something larger, but there's nothing nearby. I give up and use the pry bar from my suit instead. I unclip it from my calf and gently push one end into the light. There's resistance as soon as I do so, a heaviness far greater than that of water. Giving up on waving it right to left I try to withdraw it instead. At first I tug too hard and there's no give, but with a slower effort I find I can ease the pry bar out again.

Once outside it doesn't appear damaged, but there's some force being exerted that I can't identify. All I know for sure is that I'm keeping clear. I doubt I'd be strong enough to haul myself out again. I recall the odd burst of movement in the room back by the tree, one that occurred only when the light was off, and a thought strikes me.

Could this be a stasis field? Something only theorised by human scientists so far as I've heard but... Whatever was in that last one, it had seemed frozen in time – caught between one moment and the next. It could explain why the movement that occurred in the darkness was so immediate.

'Or could be any number of other things,' I tell myself before I get carried away. 'None of them matter so keep going.'

Rather than think, I just obey my inner captain – the only question is, which direction do I go? Has the light come on just to make me notice that side passage or was it random? Something's tried to kill me already, do I want to be following directions so placidly?

'Is this a message from the spider to the fly?' I mutter,

looking from one path to the next. 'Or a helping hand? Seems a convoluted way to get me to blunder into a trap.'

Put that way, it's a bit hard to swallow. There must be all manner of ways to damage my suit if you can control systems like that stasis field. It won't take much concerted effort before the soft bag of flesh inside doesn't stand a chance.

I decide to trust my luck – not something that's ever been hugely abundant over the years, but we're down to luck and judgement. The side passage hopefully takes me slightly more in the direction I've been aiming, so that's as good a reason as any. My suit lights seem to emphasise the close, cramped nature but other than one section where a long lump protrudes from the wall, I walk with ease down it.

Turning a corner, I find myself following an identical passage until I come to a largish open section that's been brutalised by fighting. There are narrow weapon-impact marks all over the far wall, chunks blown loose from corners and furrows in the metal floor. I'm no soldier but I can recognise a choke-point easily enough and someone clearly decided to stand their ground here. Whether it worked is anyone's guess, but I continue cautiously for one short section before it abruptly opens up ahead of me.

There's a large space and it's not entirely black, that's all I can see for the time being. I cut my suit lights and peer around the last corner. It takes me a while to comprehend what I'm seeing but when I do, I gasp.

The space isn't just large, it's enormous. I could be at the base of a city block back home, the central districts that are multi-tiered, interwoven complexes. What's ahead of me is only a short diamond-shape section of floor; fifty metres long, but with a tall central pillar section of tubes and an awkward set of blocks that zig-zag up alongside that.

I wait a while, but everything looks still so I turn my lights back on. There's absolutely no movement that I can see and, in the end, the suit lamps don't win me a whole lot extra. How far up this shaft goes I can't really guess, but it has to be several hundred metres. There are smaller tree-like spreads around this on multiple levels, some glowing faintly but partly subsumed by the outer wall so the trunk is just a bulge behind the network of nests.

The outer wall isn't blank either. There's clearly a honeycomb of rooms within and a few of those are lit up by what I suspect are more stasis fields. I stand at the base, clear of the multiple bridges that span sides and levels, and marvel at it all. The stasis fields form a patchwork like this is some sort of three-dimensional game laid out ahead of me.

I push up to the nearest and look inside. Again it's empty, but from there I see a rear chamber across the way that's lit with that strange lambent light. I cross to the window of the dark outer room and anchor myself with a hand-hold, thirty metres above the nominal ground. While I want a better view I decide against going inside. There's no doorway, just an open window section and long banks of something running all the way across the room.

Beyond it, the lit-up room has an extra-wide doorway. Through that I can see a shape similar to the other nightmare I saw. This one is low to the ground and broad with tendrils of barbed limbs stretched out, odd bulbous lumps on what appears to be its top. None of it seems to correspond to a head, eyes or mouth – just the mess of something not reflective where its body should be and a trio of massive thorns or claws at the end of several limbs.

I shiver and move on, my initial fear subsiding. With controlled bursts of movement I can hop from one section to another, ascending faster than I would if I was just walking up the side of the central column. I test to see if that's possible and my boots can't get a lock, but there are plenty of hand holds and jutting sections. I don't want to use my jets if I can help it, not in the dark with an unknown distance yet to travel.

It's a relatively easy journey, each push taking me just six or seven metres. In the darkness it's easy to go too fast and catch yourself on something, but they drill that into you pretty hard when you learn wreck-diving. Aside from pausing whenever I come close to a lit-up room, checking for threats, I continue steadily all the way up.

At the top there are larger nest-like protrusions, almost like viewing platforms, and I reach one without incident. A check of my rough map suggests it doesn't matter which way I go, but one of the platforms has significant damage and it looks like there's more in the room beyond it. I'm approximately a third of the way up the wreck, but exactly how deep the ripped-open section is, I've no idea. From what I saw from the shuttle, I'd guess at a few hundred metres, but if it exposed a shaft like this there could be more than half a kilometre of open space.

I head into the darkness of the other side and down a slope to a strangely curved corridor. It opens up ahead of me and I discover a great oval room, forty metres high with sloped tiers around most of the sides and ceiling. There's a platform in the centre and a blunt end ahead of me from which a long teardrop extends out almost to the platform. It's supported only by thin pillars and seems temporary, almost like an art installation but for the fact it's a dully smooth and featureless metal like the walls.

The room feels like a theatre but for that teardrop intruding on the space. I inspect the floor of each tier and there are seams there, regular shapes and small depressions that my imagination decides is stored seating of some type. Spaceships are practical things after all. Even on one this size that must sustain a community, every square metre of space has to be accounted for by the designers.

I continue on, plodding or drifting through the depths depending on which seems safest. Largely the wreck consists of branching tunnels and walkways. Only a few times do I have to backtrack as I find myself suddenly at a dead end of small rooms. The stasis fields, assuming that's what they are, become few and far between.

When I reach an open section that could be a city plaza, I see two – one occupied by a nightmare shape half-hidden by what seems to be complex lab equipment, the other empty. The main route there takes me to a spherical room even bigger than the theatre; glass-fronted viewing stations occupying much of the outside and a complex network of struts on the interior. The largest of those connect the sides to a small core, but there are several hundred and the majority crisscross the open space. There are oval apertures in the wall too, four large gaps that face each other and I decide this to be some sort of sporting arena. It reminds me of games I've seen played on the larger orbitals and low-g colonies.

Where I can, I travel upwards. There are many transport tubes standing dead and useless throughout the wreck. I start to find more that travel the horizontal too – not wide open rails like I saw near the shuttle bays but smaller ones. Fortunately the species that built this ship were clearly mobile and active, able to climb far better than humans so I have plenty of opportunities to head up.

There are bursts of what I assume is normal lighting – sometimes a whole section illuminates with fitful washes of sickly, green-tinted light. I scuttle for the darkness like a cockroach when that happens, but nothing tries to kill me and the longest I have to shiver in the shadows is a few minutes.

For a while at least, I begin to believe that there's nothing here other than malfunctioning systems triggering at random.

11

As I continue, the landscape of this dead and dark place evolves around me. Hidden in the shadows are flourishes absent from lower levels. A sculptor's hand in corridors and walls, intricate symbols and flowing shapes. I feel traces of a caste system or other hierarchy reaching out like ghostly hands, brushing my awareness as I walk or float. It grows increasingly difficult to remember I'm inside a wrecked ship. The scale is simply staggering. It feels more like a vast necropolis where most are resting peacefully, but for a few glimpsed spirits frozen in uneasy limbo.

Time passes, slow and wearying. My Heads-Up Display has a mission clock tucked away in the corner of my visor. I don't need to pay much attention to it, not yet, but it begins to prey on my mind so I switch off the view. I've been in here for almost four hours, but in the stillness that feels far longer. I'm not hungry or tired yet, I'll happily walk all day long out on vacation with the family, but that's also at the back of my mind. Terror will tire you faster and fatigue breeds mistakes. I've got a long way to travel before I reach the likely hazardous tear that killed this ship.

When I reach what seems to be a frozen lake, I begin to get the sense I'm not entirely alone. The lake seems to be part of some embedded ecosystem running through the ship, judging from the network of pipes and surrounding halo of what I guess is hydroponic chambers. I imagine them as the fossilised seeds of some vast flower, all connected to the lake in the centre. Now they're just interlinked rooms choked with dust and dirt, maybe a few desiccated bones if we're lucky.

I dare not go into any of those, but the scraps I can see in the darkness suggest a remarkable complexity. The lake itself is a murky, misshapen growth in a bowl-shaped chamber contained by airlocks. I walk through blast doors that have been ripped open, glide across the glittering, ancient ice. Like the round chamber I've dubbed the sports arena, there are viewing ports all over. The glow of one stasis field lends a sense of proportion to the place and it's in one of the other windows I detect or imagine a faint movement in the shadows.

The drift of light, brief stutters of shapes. It gives me a jolt and my heart hammers loud in my ears, but then they're gone. I can't even tell if I'm imagining things. Everything returns to dark again, everything is still. If I'm going to lose my mind it'll be somewhere like this, I remind myself.

I move faster, telling myself it's only jitters. Leaving the lake behind I find a short shaft to climb, blank walls on either side. At the top it looks like I'm standing on house-sized building blocks, nine in all and assembled in a square. Unusually there are no hand-holds or exits that I can see, only smooth surfaces. Guessing I've wandered off the path, I spend a while scouting for exits and finally find one on the far side, a small access shaft like the first one I used. That takes me to somewhere just as strange – a long, low avenue lined with identical blocks. Each one is almost two metres high with intricate markings and what appears to be a crystalline powder leaks from most. It hangs glittering in the void where I disturb it, so I hurry carefully on, open doorway after open doorway returning me to the more familiar-style thoroughfares.

Even then things remain strange. I find myself in rooms of columns each bearing a spray of eighteen flower-like pods large enough for a child to sleep in. There are swirling designs engraved into many of the surfaces, some obscured by blast- and blade-damage but most still beautiful with cryptic abstraction. It makes me think of my children when they were little; the snug, smooth-edged crib we used.

A wave of sadness hits me, makes me falter. From some precious corner of my memory my nose is suddenly full of the scent of my son, Elam, as a baby. My shoulder can feel the press of his tiny sleeping body and the cloth he was wrapped in. I picture his smile and his sister's too. Imah, so serious, so focused compared to her brother, but when she smiles it can power ships.

It's only been a couple of weeks since I saw them last, but at that moment I feel the distance between us. The vastness of the great dark that is just an engine failure away from being an impossible gulf. I stop and sit on a raised block, too distracted to even test it first. Sitting makes no difference of course, not in zero-g, but part of me needs to all the same.

It's not an entirely alien feeling. Most spacers get it the first time they set foot on a different planet. The dislocation. The sense of mind-blowing distances that aren't so real when you're in your ship, surrounded by the familiar. You need a moment to gather your wits, to find yourself again amid the huge emptiness that's filled your mind. Without the mission clock I can't time it, but after a few minutes the captain's part of my brain declares it's time to get back to work.

I rise with a sigh and something in my suit beeps – the monitoring system that ensures you're healthy. I give a verbal command and open my mouth, waiting for a thin tube to pop forward from the suit. From that I swallow down something blandly tasteless, hardly a reviving cup of coffee but the simple action serves as a reminder. I've got a goal, my suit still functions, I'm going to get back to the ship. I'm going to find a way.

Surrounded by the dust of dead things, the shapes of their souls hanging in the air, I remind myself to keep going. The guilt about Kall is a weight dragging at my heel, slowing me down, but I've got to be cold-hearted there. Mourning and regret can only be useful to the living and I mean to live.

All of a sudden, I get another glimpse of movement through the crib-rooms. This time I know I'm not imagining it. There's a flash of gold and then nothing, a sense of movement but no more. Worryingly the motion sensor remains silent. I check it's functioning and it seems to be, but whatever glimpse I'm getting isn't enough to set it off. Before I can react there's another blink of white light from elsewhere. Still nothing from the tracker but I see it more clearly this time even if my brain struggles to recognise it.

A figure in motion. Shorter than me, long limbs moving with sharp urgency. Turning away? Six limbs?

In the next second it's gone, winked out of existence and swallowed by the blackness. This time I pursue however, half in a dream. My terror remains, but that's mostly reserved for the lightless horrors. Things you would not see coming, designed to drink in the light and be undetected in the shadows. This glimpse is ghostly but more familiar and my fear is all used up by the unknown.

When I reach the place I saw it, there is of course nothing. I continue – suddenly consumed by two ideas simultaneously, that I have a saviour and a hunter. I cannot bear the idea of being pursued, not here, so I go in search of this phantom. Through one broad doorway I enter a narrow street, a communal space with rooms leading off on two levels but only forty metres long. Again, I glimpse something in the shadows, vanishing up an incline. It leads me to a succession of large, low rooms partitioned by sections of intricate, glittering fretwork.

I pursue with a mounting sense of being led by the nose. Finally when I come to a massive domed hall with concentric crystalline rings, I stop. There is an exit, but I don't see how whatever I'm pursuing would have had time to reach it. Not at a speed I'd been keeping up with, albeit at the edge of sight. And yet there's nothing here. Either there are hiding places in here, I'm making the whole thing up, or it's capable of outpacing me at will. None of those conclusions are reassuring and I stop to assess my options.

The map projected by my suit suggests I'm fairly close to my destination. The pursuit hasn't taken me off-course, assuming the suit's system was accurate in fixing a location to start with. It flickers as I bring it up and I feel a stab of fear before it stabilises. The wreck is so vast I'm impossibly lost by now – only this rough plan is keeping me sane. Even trying to follow a general direction, the irregular turns and angles would have thrown me well off course without it.

After a few moments thought I decide to back-track, looking for an alternative exit. I investigate one doorway and discover it leads through to a series of narrow rooms. Fortunately those open into another crossroad with transport tubes in the centre. There I can climb almost fifty metres using hand-holds and exit through a wide corridor.

It's only when I move well beyond that, looking for the next tube or shaft to ascend, that I discover a problem. A very large room is my only option, sub-divided into square plots by wide corner-section pillars. I guess at a few hundred plots, most empty but many with blocks of all shapes and sizes in the centre. I cross it feeling oddly exposed, surrounded by both long empty stretches and plentiful hiding spaces.

At the far end, the room narrows and becomes a wide bifurcated corridor curving around a rounded platform at head height. It's just enough to obscure my view of what's beyond but my heart still falls before I'm round it because I see the glow. Sure enough, though there are four antechambers leading away, each one is blocked by a glowing stasis field.

I stare at them a while, mind blank about what to do. Before turning back I test them with a disintegrating set of round-cornered cubes I find nearby. Each stasis field absorbs the block and holds it just a few centimetres from the edge. I may be wrong about what the glowing field is, but not about whether I want to go in there.

I go back, retracing my steps when I stop dead. There's a pinging sound in my ear, pitched to catch my attention and pulsing like a fast heartbeat. The motion tracker. I look wildly around, lights sweeping the room, but can see nothing.

'Overlay tracker,' I order the suit's Heads-Up Display, dimming the lamps so I can follow it better. As I scan around, I spot the movement. Slow, laboured but purposeful. I struggle to make out the shape even with the traced outline of the tracker and then I realise why – it's one of the light-absorbing nightmares. Only this time it's not frozen in stasis, it's stalking the halls.

I recoil instinctively. The movement catches its notice and it whips around, one long arm curled around a pillar. Then it spots me and hurls itself carelessly forward. I stagger back, mind momentarily drowned in terror, as it clatters soundlessly against the next pillar. Some of the tentacle-arms hang limp. Pieces actually tear off when they catch the floor or pillar, but not enough for my liking. I lurch away as it ricochets off another pillar, ribbons of perfectly black almost-flesh streaming behind it as it spins sideways.

Briefly I look at the harpoon gun, but I'm not confident in the one shot I have left. I edge back, retreating towards the stasis fields with some vague notion that even a non-lethal hit might drive the thing into one. That would give me space to get away, but as I near them I realise there's no way to ambush it. In zero-g the thing could just go over the platform. I've no way of getting the angle I need. Still I retreat, instinct driving me away to buy time.

Eventually I've got my back to one of the middle fields. I can almost imagine a static hiss, but the only sound is the intermittent pulse of the motion tracker. It goes into active mode when it picks up an oncoming target, firing out light pulses in all directions to assemble a map of the surrounding area.

Out of the corner of my visor I see the stasis fields as dead space, blank walls that don't reflect the pulses at all. By contrast a 3-D abstraction has overlaid the platform ahead, a flailing mass of thin limbs surging up behind it. As it slams against the far side it pauses, searching, and I release my boot-locks. Floating just above the floor, I ready my manoeuvring jets. With luck this thing will be a bundle of instinct and fury – as much as it looks anyway. If it hurls itself at me, I may be able to dodge and let it go straight into the stasis field.

It starts to claw its way over, reaching the top of the platform in a second. My vision is a mess of outlines and shadows, bleached to grey by the suit lamps. Only then do I notice something's different. The light has dimmed. The glow of the stasis fields. I turn, fearful of looking away but desperate to. There it is; an empty room right where I'm standing.

One of the stasis fields has disappeared – switched off or something. I'm caught in a moment of confusion, not knowing whether to trust it. The random lashing of limbs ahead makes the decision for me, terror forcing me to act. I tap the control pad of my suit and zip backwards. Nothing stops or slows me. I'm through in a few seconds.

The motion tracker continues to blare, ever more insistent as the nightmare scrambles on. It appears over the edge of the platform and doesn't stop, pushing off without a moment's pause. I release the jet controls and raise my harpoon, straighten the arm so the jet on my shoulder can compensate for the kick. But before I can fire there's a judder as though the vacuum itself has been grabbed in a vice and crushed.

The overlay of the motion tracker shudders and fractures, unable to display what its sensors are saying. My eyes blur too, both from a sudden burst of light and the movement. And then just like that, with shocking speed, all is still. The stasis field has returned and the nightmare hangs most of the way inside it, frozen. As for the rest, the few trailing limbs that didn't make it in before the field returned, they're limp and drifting like a dead thing.

The motion tracker goes silent. All I can hear is the sound of my frantic breathing, the hammer of my heart inside the air bubble of my suit. And then another single ping from the tracker. This time from behind me. Almost too scared to move, I turn around.

12

Behind me there's a ghost. Not a flickering spectral image. Not some half-seen figure moving through the darkness, but something both better and worse. A living creature. Or rather, what remains of one. All that's left behind when life is gone and the body decays.

The room isn't large, but it's imposing. An ovoid pod sits in the centre with two tall openings in its flanks, through which I can see the ghost. On the left is some sort of large upright hemisphere bowl with hexagonal shapes protruding from the inner face while on the right stands a half-circle of ring-shaped workstations. There's no damage to the rest of the room but the pod has been torn and smashed into a dozen times or more. Chunks have been gouged out, deep scoring runs across all the flanks, but that's not the shocking part. The shock is the ghost inside.

The pale glow of a stasis field fills the interior of the pod. As before it doesn't extend beyond the bounds, though this is just a few metres across instead of an entire room. And inside that stasis field is something long dead, hazy and diffuse in the air.

I can't make out exactly what it is, just the shape of where it had been. Upright and six-limbed, torso twisting slightly away from me as one of its large upper limbs reaches high. Its constituent parts have disintegrated, expanding as slowly as a star-chart. There's a smear of green, a suggestion of red where once clothing might have been. The head has no face, no structure either. Only a longer, less substantial sweep at the sides where perhaps hair or elongated ears might have been.

A constellation is all that remains. I fight the urge to circle it, to move around in search of a point where that dust-cloud puzzle resolves into a coherent image. There's one thing that is clear enough still, either a more recent addition or more resistant to the effects of time and stasis that are nevertheless starting to have the same effect. A long thorny branch of darkness has been driven right inside.

It's broken off roughly and I can get close enough to see a grey lattice-like endoskeleton within its light-drinking skin. Organic or machine, I still can't tell. The skin too is flaking into nothingness – resisting the effects but not for much longer. I can see it better now and realise the black is not absolute. There's a very faint, elusive speckling to it, like the further stars on a moonless night. Barely visible, easy to dismiss as imaginary, and somehow adding to the depthless, texture-less impression it gives.

I look back at the tangle of fury caught in the moment before it killed me. It is not missing a limb but there can be no doubt what sort of thing killed this ghost – or attempted to.

But if they disintegrate over time, why bother?

I don't get an answer to my question, but it still troubles me. There's a malice in all this – ingrained and heedless of injury. Either it knew it would have to rip itself free of the stasis field or it was so savagely mindless it could not hold back.

In my shock I realise I've forgotten about that sensor ping. I start forward then stop again, unsure where I could go. I edge towards the great hemisphere. It's set into the wall so free of hiding places at least. The hexagonal protrusions only stick out twenty centimetres or so. I take a few steps with the harpoon raised then falter as my helmet lights reveal the wide doorway on the other side of the central pod. It's open and beyond it I can see a far larger room. If there's a threat anywhere, it could most easily come from that direction.

I go to the doorway and assess the black space beyond. There's dust and debris everywhere, shuttle-size objects seemingly lashed together or locked in some sort of crazed struggle. The chaotic tangle makes it hard to make out any one part, but it's certainly not a room I want to pass through much. With or without my jets, manoeuvring a path through the mess will be difficult at best.

While I'm trying to decide what to do, I see new flickers of light, far on the other side. It seems to be tiered, reminding me of rice terraces with organic, flowing lines, one rising above the next again and again. On one of those terraces, well above the floor of the room, two lights move.

Two figures – blurred, jagged in movement and visible just for a few seconds. Then more lights. Stuttering bursts from above and below that seem to be going in the same direction before the rounded lip of dozens of terraces join it. This light has no consistency though, no clear direction. It's as though the light itself is fighting the dark, thrashing furiously to penetrate the shadows only to be stymied again and again.

After a short while, ten seconds at most, all falls dark again. The only light is the icy beam of my EVA suit, lighting up the particles in the air, and the weak glow of the stasis field that casts so little beyond its bounds. I check all around in case I've been dumb and missed something, but the walls remain featureless and solid – the way I came even less of an option.

Giving up, I edge forward into the large chamber, trying to get a sense of it. It's hard to make out through the myriad obstacles, but the ceiling doesn't seem flat. Instead it's curved. I remind myself that I'm still trying to go up, to find shafts and the like that'll take me that way. Here seems a good opportunity for just that but there's so much debris I'm struggling to work out how.

The nearest piece is a broken machine of some kind hovering just a metre off the floor. As a test, I shove it upwards with the EVA suit's augmented strength, wondering if I can clear a path. It strikes several things, twisting and lashing back at me with a spray of cables that barely miss my head. More objects move, spinning and colliding in a dizzying display I can barely keep track of. They crash into others and soon there are objects moving in all directions, many with dangerous edges slashing through the vacuum.

I retreat to the pod, my ghost-friend now less alarming than the chaos I've sparked out there. While I'm thinking about what to do my motion tracker chirrups again and my heart leaps into my throat. My harpoon is up before I even think about it as a section of the wall swings forward. I set myself, ready to fire if something dark and thorn-like bursts through, but instead the tracker falls silent once again. I edge sideways, hoping to use the pod to hide behind if something does hurl itself out. Instead of something coming to kill me however, a panel on the wall flickers and an elegant script appears there, pale green. A word.

—hello—

13

The wall has just said "hello" to me. Honestly it's not even at the top of the list for weird shit happening to me, but still I can't even work out how to react. Mostly I fail and just stare blankly at my new friend, the wall. Sheer surprise makes me lower the harpoon at least.

'Hello, wall?' I say, nervous exhaustion making me very silly all of a sudden. I mean, the wall can't hear me, there's no air for the words to travel through. Still, it's the friendliest thing I've encountered here so far and I feel I should make the effort.

It doesn't reply. After a few moments the words disappear and I feel a touch of disappointment and worry, but that all vanishes a second later. A figure steps out from behind the wall and I give a little shriek. It's unlike the horrors roaming these halls, unlike anything except...

I look back towards the pod, the six-limbed ghost within it. Then up and around at the ship, remembering the view from outside. The figure before me, poised cautiously at the end of the wall panel, isn't biological but follows the same configuration. Some form of ship servitor I imagine, built for mindless labour but with unusual elegance to the craftsmanship. It's gunmetal grey shot through with silver and gold, just like the ship itself. There are a few discordant sections I notice, some black, others lighter grey or white. Replacement pieces I imagine, but all from the same design.

The robot stands on two legs but could easily drop to all six. The middle limbs are short and delicate, a child's arm compared to the adult legs of its other four. Each hand/foot has three digits, flatter than human fingers but a similar length with two broad thumbs flanking a single index.

Its head is small with flattened sides, narrowing to the front. When it turns I realise it's the same at the back with four eyes on each side, binocular vision in all directions. It has a quizzical air as it inspects me and I wonder what to do next.

'Hello,' I say again, before my brain catches up and my gut jolts. This isn't just a servitor – it can't be. Not in a wreck this broken, with fitful power to run a central network.

Howling dark, it said "hello" to me. Something here has received and decoded the contact package!

'You're some sort of AI-linked avatar?' I say, more to myself than the machine that can't hear me.

I don't understand what's going on now. There's comms capability and serious processing power at work here. That's the only way it can have written a human word and yet...

How's a ship with all that still here – abandoned in space and looking for all the universe like a dead wreck? If even part of the ship's still viable, how is anything still here after all this time? And what is it that's been trying to kill me? Some sort of rogue security response? Is the AI corrupted? Is this all some deranged, discordant reaction to my arrival? But if it's so broken, how could it access the contact package?

'Shut up, Song,' I tell myself. 'There's only one way you'll get answers – by asking this thing. And that means you have to find a way to reply.'

I pause, racking my brains for an answer and cursing the designers of my fancy EVA suit who didn't think to include a bloody pen. It makes my heart ache for the sound of anything other than my own breathing and the faint clack of my boots on metal. The sound of my children's voices, the clatter of a mealtime.

It's just been a few hours, but the oppression of no sound is starting to wear me down. Even the idle background chatter of a computer or vid from a crewmate's room would be heavenly right now. Absently I deactivate the motion tracker that's pinging in my ear and try to concentrate on the matter at hand.

I've got a diamond-edge cutter and lots of handy floor, but that'll be slow – quite aside from how a ship's droid might react. I check my suit interface which automatically reacts to display the rough plan of the ship I have. The avatar/servitor reacts immediately – not as a biological would but enough for a twitch and readjust to display interest. The word on the wall is replaced with another.

—ship—

I nod and skip through commands, trying to find some sort of sufficiently-simple text log. I drag one out and activate it. An afterthought from the suit manufacturers no doubt. Probably just some junior designer tinkering with the already-present comms capabilities, but it's there. I just need to remember to limit what I say out loud. The last thing a potentially momentous first-contact situation needs is every thought that crosses my mind.

Finally it's ready – enlarged and reversed so I can raise

the field like a transparent shield between us and display a reply.

"Hello"

—injury yes/no—

"No"

—alone yes/no—

I feel that like a stab to the gut.

"Yes. No. My friend... he died. There was an accident or something soon after we arrived. I had to leave him... I... I left him behind."

I stop, trying to quell the emotion inside me. The avatar just stares at me, unmoving.

—dead—

I choke briefly as I allow myself to picture Kall's body. "Yes – killed by our drone when it turned on us."

—new friend yes/no—

"You? I... I hope so. Yes"

There's a pause as the avatar digests this. I don't know how to react as it waits. I've only ever conversed with a limited-personality AI back home or on board a large ship. The *Sak* is a clear order below that even. The fully-sentient AIs are rare and colossally powerful – intellect combined with vast processing power in a world of networks – so they don't have much need of someone like me. I don't even know if there's one on the ruling council of my employers, the Filerich Conglomerate. Half of what I know comes from probably-fanciful fiction media, the rest being my poor recollection of school.

They all should run faster than a human brain though, cycling through hundreds of options before I've processed a single word. Does the pause mean this one is damaged? Co-ordinating with another? Maybe this is a servitor after all, just linked to an AI and receiving commands through some jury-rigged system perhaps.

The very question makes me anxious. I don't know much about AIs and right now that's a concern. I can't tell how they'll react, how they'll view me.

—friend— the avatar seems to conclude. I breathe a sigh of relief.

"Do... do you have a name?"

—name yes/no—

This throws me slightly, but there could be a number of reasons for confusion here. I think for a moment then try another track.

"You are connected to this ship?"

—some times—

"There is danger here?"

—danger yes— it replies with a firmness I might be imagining. The avatar raises one large upper arm and points back towards the nightmare that had been pursuing me.

"Many?" I ask.

–937—

"That's... oh hells, that's a lot." I look at the thing that had chased me. "What are they?"

–danger: weapons: hunters—

"How long have you been here?"

—unknown scale: second minute hour day year—

I'm silent for a while, trying to work out how I'd even describe the period of time involved. There's the standard measurement based on the rotational period of a planet I've never even visited, but exactly how long any of that is... my school days return to me only hazily, but I'm sure it involves the vibration of atoms somewhere.

"I've been on this ship..." I pause to check my mission log, "approximately five point three hours."

There's a short pause.

—time elapsed estimate: one hundred thirty-four thousand, two hundred six years—

I gape. Especially given the short window most species have in their end-stages, that was a long damn time ago. How this wreck is still holding orbit is nothing short of miraculous. In the next moment I feel a stab of sympathy for my new friend.

"You've been alone for one hundred and thirty-four thousand years?"

—potential estimate error: yes—

"Alone?"

—limited survivors: environment failure: target core units: final loss attack plus three years—

"I... are you sentient?"

It's not a question I want to ask much. It's easier to think of a servitor inhabiting this place, heedless of time. Even a limited AI would surely go mad stuck somewhere so utterly empty and dead, but the avatar doesn't react the way I'd expect a general system to.

—sentient yes: high functions restricted: preservation protocols—

The ache in my gut increases, my guilt momentarily replaced with sympathy. They have been forced to disable their personality to survive the millennia. The choice of insanity or a strange drawn-out purgatory, the loss of self but not a stasis sleep. Something else. Something that likely retained some glimpse of what was lost.

My head spins as I consider how that must have been, but I force myself to focus.

"Can you show me how to get out?"

—out yes—

"I..."

I pause and bring up the rough plan I have of the wreck – probably laughably bad and incomplete to a being that knows it far better than I'll ever know the *Sakakawea*. With my free hand I point at the torn section I've been aiming for. It looks like I'm most of the way there, but the suit is using estimates and I've no idea how direct a path I've got left.

"Here? Out?"

—here danger— the avatar replies, edging forward to inspect my plan but maintaining contact with the wall still.

It looks almost shy, nervous of the stranger. I remind myself that every human-built servitor or avatar could rip me limb from limb should they choose.

"Many?"

—many—

My heart sinks and the strength drains out of me. A wide open section patrolled by those things? I wouldn't stand a chance.

"Is there another way?"

—out to a ship yes/no—

"Yes! My ship, waiting out there!"

—others like you yes/no—

"Yes. Something disabled our communications but they'll be looking for me."

—communications are danger—

"I know. That's how Kall died. Our drone tried to kill us after we lost comms. But some of my friends are still out there, waiting"

—I go out yes/no—

"You... You want to come too?" I don't know why it catches me off guard, but somehow the question does. I blink for a while then nod. What else can I do if I want to survive? Tell them they have to remain in purgatory another few thousand years? How else could I treat any sentient being?

"Yes. You and me go out. There's room on my ship for us all."

—I wake— the avatar gives a faint shudder then gives a scooping gesture that I guess is beckoning.

—you follow: danger come here—

With that they vanish back behind the wall panel.

14

Left with just an empty room and the prospect of danger arriving, I don't contemplate what might be behind the wall panel for long. I check the manual safety catch on my harpoon is off because I'm not a total idiot, then edge around it. My helmet lamps illuminate a small cavity running through the wall – a service channel for bots most likely. Lightless, awkward, and cramped, it's far more like the less-than-pristine corridors of the first ship I served on. I have to restrain myself from running towards the familiar.

I take care all the same as I work myself into the space. The EVA suit barely fits. I have to crab along sideways and reduce my lights so the glare doesn't dazzle me, but I get in. A few metres ahead the avatar watches me until I'm comfortably in, whereupon it places a hand on a flat runner at waist-height. I'd assumed it was some sort of wiring channel but there's a glow under its palm and the wall closes behind me.

Now I start to worry, like a bloody fool. It's far too late to do anything about it, but once I'm away from that nightmare of thorns, other fears start to press in. I follow for a long while, the passageway moving through regular sharp turns. I assume it describes the shape of rooms, turning corners and ascending levels, but there are parts that don't map onto anything I see. Chicanes that might be around transport tubes except they seem to turn unexpectedly and hint at another shape entirely. Steps and ramps that peter out after just a metre or so. Random dips and troughs where the walkway bridges the gap.

On and on we go. Far enough I find myself light-headed and confused. Wondering where we're going. Wondering if this is all just a hypoxia dream. Time and again I start to call out, to raise my voice to catch their attention then remember my guide cannot hear me. Unable to catch them as they nimbly weave their way, fearful of stopping and being left behind, I tramp on – careful to avoid my armoured shoulders catching the sides.

I fall into something of a trance, hypnotised by the steady walk, lulled by the unchanging view. Or driven by the entombing walls into drawing deep within myself, blocking out the physical. I think of Jamal, of my children, their faces and their smiles. Hardly the perfect family, but the sum total of my love these days. No place I'd rather be now. This wreck is a risk I've taken for them, to stop it all from spiralling away, but now more than ever I'd gladly give it up. Trade my claim to just be back on the *Sakakawea*, watching the lights as we streak though sub-space towards home.

Sien Nau is a place of sunset and shadow – canyons and surging rivers. The middle zone of our oddly tilted planet where the sun rarely creeps halfway up the sky. Blue sky is a rare thing for us, we move between orange-red and night through most of our year. I'm drawn back to that place now, enclosed and half-seen things evoking a sense of home. A sense of all I'm desperate for.

After more than half an hour of walking we emerge into a high chamber. The avatar moves confidently, apparently certain there is no danger here, but I'm still cautious. I edge out, unable to see much at first as shadows yaw and turn under my dim lights. When I restore them to full power I see we are in another tree room, not identical but broadly similar. Like a religious icon created by a master-artist from a different era, but equally as beautiful.

Or it once was. This one is darker with most branches broken off. The pieces hang shattered in the vacuum, abandoned in a chaotic jumble. The stub of one branch reaches towards us. It's in a hundred pieces or more, but each is fixed in its proper place. With a gap between each, it's an exploded view of how the tree once looked.

As I stare around in wonder, the avatar leaves me and goes to fetch another piece. As large as their torso, the avatar manoeuvres it with ease, pushing gently up towards the matching broken stump. Using all four upper limbs they bring it gently into position. Only now do I see a narrow pin jutting from the stump – some clear material about ten centimetres long. With that to bridge the gap they manoeuvre the piece into position, hold for a short while then delicately disengage. That done they simply leave it in place and turn away.

A subtle piece of art? I wonder, staring up at the reassembled limbs. *Or something more practical?*

I realise now almost all the existing branches had once been broken. Each brought back together by the avatar no doubt and held by near-invisible pins. A subversive act perhaps – one designed for only the avatar themself and the dull, slavering nightmares that stalk these halls. Would those notice such a thing? A reassembly of what they must have broken once, performed so gradually they could not comprehend it?

Or is this something more tragic and futile? A compulsion to rebuild in the vain hope life can be restored?

The avatar doesn't look so unthinking though, as they come towards me. That one piece done, they're content to leave off. A stone added to the cairn each time they pass. They watch me in their curious, angled way for a while. I have no idea what they're thinking, whether I'm even the subject of their thoughts, but eventually they collect a slanted shard of the broken tree and hold it up. It's imperfect but strangely beautiful as words light up on it – the material as reactive as the wall panel it appears.

—safe here— it displays in the same whitest shade of green.

I fiddle briefly with my own display, feeling encumbered and as awkward as a child though I'm not the one having to fetch up scrap before talking.

"How do you know? Can you track those things?"

—no: sensors non-functional: pattern flow obstacles—

I think for a moment.

"Obstacles? You use the stasis fields?"

—yes: game/model/prediction—

"Game?" I exclaim.

Even as I do so it makes a sort of sense though. The nightmares seem limited, running on simple parameters that make them easily outwitted. But if that's the case, how hasn't the avatar done so in all the years they've been here? Even with a few thousand to contend with, they'd only need to trap/disable one every few years to be done by now. Unless...

"Who are you playing the game against? Those thorn-machines or something else?"

—star-thorns: physical assault units: pieces on board: opponent non-physical—

"Where?"

—everywhere-all systems—

With that the final pieces fall into place for me. The hangar door trying to kill me, the unknown signal that popped my comms and turned my drone against me. Not some automated defence system, certainly not a ghost. Instead a component of the assault that tore into this ship all those thousands of years ago, one that could wreak havoc once inserted by the physical assault units.

"A weaponised virus," I realise. "Autonomous and directing the... star-thorns, you called them?

—yes—

"Is the virus sentient?"

—no—

"But made to kill? Why hasn't it destroyed the ship?"

—made to kill biological sentients: programmed to capture ship's core / connected artificial sentients—

"You."

—yes—

"It's been hunting you for thousands of years? I doubt the civilisation it serves even exists now."

—probability low: probability high war is ended: probability high both species functionally extinct—

"Except for you," I finish.

—alone— the avatar agrees. —war ended: defeated: eradicated—

My heart aches once more. "But you're still here. Still alive after all this time."

—memory records remain: final memorial—

There's a pause as their head twitches towards the shattered tree in a strangely human way.

—defeat not final: war continues here—

"You don't want to lose this war, even after all this time? Even after it stopped mattering to anyone but you?"

—no—

Despite myself I smile. It's crazed, stupid, insanely stubborn and probably exactly what I'd have done too. Jamal always said I was too competitive, but I don't agree. With the kids I can let it go; I've never been one of those parents keen to prove mastery over their offspring. But with others – adults, in trade or sport, hells yes I want to win. If I'd seen everyone I knew slaughtered, I'd want to outlast the fucks who did it. Maybe even if that mean shutting my brain down and existing in limbo for thousands of years until my opportunity came.

"How do you win this war? Destroy them?"

—escape—

I nod. "In that case, we may be able to help each other." I stick out a hand. "My name is Song."

15

—Name Song— they repeat back, inspecting the proffered hand.

Before I feel too awkward they make a decision and take it in one of their own. The large double-thumbs fold around my hand and make it jiggle.

That's what you get when you're working off dictionary definitions, I think, inwardly amused at the sight of my hand being shaken.

The contact package has a vast amount of information, most of which being context to understand words. That the avatar is talking to me at all is an indication of exceptional processing power. Only the rare, true-sentient AIs on human worlds would be able to do it so quickly.

Without fully appreciating it, I note their language has improved just in the time we've been talking. Part of their "brain" is still processing, refining how to use the contact package information.

Are they still waking up too? Is this them still working at a limited speed?

Then something new appears on the fragment they're holding.

—name Ulu—

"Ulu?"

—approximation: incomplete descriptors: removing biological limitation incompatibility: acceptable temporary selection—

Hah – I only met this alien a short while ago and they're already mocking my species' limitations.

"Ulu it is then," I say. "Nice to meet you."

—great joy of your arrival—

Oh you say the sweetest things, I manage not to say out loud. "So how do we get out?" I ask instead.

Ulu turns the panel flat and a projection flickers to life above it. I can't help but gasp – as much at the difference between it and mine. The image is of the ship we're standing in, that much is recognizable. But it begins as an original view, straight off the factory line as it were, then battle damage is added, then sections darken both within and on the vast hull. Tiny writing appears briefly before winking out again; annotations I imagine, written in some sort of gorgeous three-dimensional script that looks almost like flowers.

A large section, running through the core of the entire ship, darkens and the projection stutters momentarily. Ulu has no face to give anything away but all the same, my heart goes out to them. I guess that was the computing core, AI heart or linking network between avatars. Whatever it was, I know that a fraction of hesitation like that to an AI that runs far faster than a human... well, the equivalent would probably be me howling with grief for the next hour.

Tiny lights start to blossom in the view. They're so small

I can barely make them out, just pinpricks that fill out some sections, but ebb and flow in others.

—stasis— the panel tells me.

I watch the movements a little longer, trying to fathom a pattern, but it's vastly complex – individual rooms within hundreds and hundreds of kilometres of internal structure.

"Your game," I reply instead.

One spot pulses red, large to attract my attention then drawing in on itself.

"Is that us?" I ask, guessing it's close to where I had been heading.

—yes—

The red light then traces a path – slow and oblique, making minute turns I can barely see – away from the great tear that had been my goal. Instead it takes me further back, towards the engines. It's a longer journey but ends up on the surface. I peer closer and Ulu obligingly zooms in the view, but still I can see nothing there. No shuttle bay, not airlock door or even a vent. Overlapping oval lines mark the translucent hull projection but there's no indication of what's there.

"I don't understand," I say at last.

—plan— Ulu replies with what feels like emphasis. It takes me a moment to realise that's because the word is displayed fractionally larger.

—escape vessel absent from ship's record—

"So the hunter virus has no record of it," I realise out loud. "It's in the main computer and can monitor the ship's systems, but if something new is built, it overlooks it."

—no: main computer erased—

I hesitate. "Destroyed in the attack? Erased by the virus?"

Ulu does not respond at first, the sheet is blank. The

moment stretches out and when they finally answer it's abrupt.

—no—

"You?"

—yes—

"I... I don't know what to say. You were a part of it? That must have been terrible."

—terrible yes: alternatives no: core gives full control of ship: non-sentient network for access core units—

"And with full control, there's nothing it couldn't do," I finish.

—core collective decision: eject main power units: burn core: disable systems: crew and inhabitants dying: could not prevent: sorrow—

I'm quiet for a long while and Ulu just stands there, perfectly still, frozen in the memories.

"You could only contain the virus?" I say at last. "Stop it from being able to use the ship. Did you know you'd be left here? Waiting for help that might never come."

—decision made in awareness— Ulu replies. —remaining avatars agree course of action: probability low of victory in war: hope—

"Hope?" I repeat, almost aghast. "The hope of rescue left you stuck here for a hundred thousand years."

—no: a choice: self-termination permitted: choice to wait after remaining avatars died—

"How did they die?"

—star-thorn units and virus: damaged/destroyed units trigger war-swarm response—

"You tried to fight and they killed the others."

—yes: separate actions: assignment failed: no damage: position overlooked during counter–attack—

"So they missed you, but wiped out all of the others.

And you've been avoiding that ever since? But the virus is contained in local systems? Could you not shut them down individually? Drive it out and restrict any co-ordinated response?"

—attempts failed: containment limited: night and day cycle—

"I don't understand."

Ulu tilts their head up at me. The gesture seems both entirely innocent and faintly pitying somehow.

—stasis fields require power: main units ejected: limited solar collection capacity: orbit maintenance required: without sun virus is free—

I look around at the freezing darkness that surrounds me. The shadows lurch in my lamp lights, the destruction seems all the more total. Even the dead are missing, disintegrated over the thousands of years and returned to stardust. It's then, in the depths of a moment of pure despondency, my suit pings its first warning about my air supply.

16

Panic surges through my veins like a hit of glitter-smoke. My vision swims, my balance wavers despite the magnetic boots. Ulu sees me waver, arms flailing, and steps forward with one hand outstretched. I grab it without thinking, desperate for any sort of anchor.

Their grip is solid – metal and unyielding power. Tugging on that arm is enough to jolt me back. Ulu could be a bulkhead of the ship for all I could move them. My thoughts clear enough to focus on the flashing corner on my HUD, the air supply indicator.

Despite the hammering of my heart, I realise it's not an emergency yet. Six hours into my air supply, I've got twenty per cent left. Normally an indicator to go back to the shuttle or summon a drone for resupply, but that option would only get me killed faster now.

Words flash up on the broken shard. I need a moment to focus on it let alone formulate a reply. The alarm has shaken me up more than it should have – uncorking the feelings I'd been keeping bottled up.

—malfunction yes/no—

"No – air supply warning," I reply. "I have an hour and a half of air left."

—nitrogen/oxygen mixture: regrets cannot supply—

"Can we get off the ship in time?"

—yes: possible launch in one hour approximate: maintain current speed: distance to ship unknown variable: escape vessel limited thrust—

"If they see us, they'll come to rescue us, I know it!"

—inside exclusion zone ship will experience systems failures: navigation shut down—

"then... wait – what?" I yell. "Systems failure? How do you know that?"

—regrets: necessary contingency—

That makes a chill run down my spine. For all Ulu's very human instinct to take my hand, this is all machine. And the old prejudices about AIs that run through humanity are not so far from the surface as I realise. I disengage and take a step back, fearful of such a loaded statement made with cold dispassion.

"Contingency?" I say at last. "What do you mean?"

Sien Nau likes to consider itself a progressive planet, certainly by the standards of most. Sentient AIs are accepted – cautiously, but given their capabilities that's only reasonable. There aren't many, however. The handful of vast-capacity AI who assist/control so much of the planet's running ruthlessly police their own. They're only half-jokingly referred to as the seven gods, after all.

However – if there's one thing that several hundred years of history, half of the planetary unions, and fiction-media writers all agree on, it's the potential for danger. It's not something anyone wants to go back to, that paranoia and suspicion, but still. The cultural fear remains.

—it is night— Ulu replies —power capacity cannot

contain virus at night: preservation of escape route necessitates restriction of proximity—

"So you disabled my bloody ship?"

—no: inserted necessary restrictions: enforce distance to preserve safety of ship—

"What about me? What about my shuttle? You let us board."

—unable to interpret/recreate language code in time period: signal sent to ship as power reserve cascade began—

"Reserve cascade? What in the hell's that?"

—power reserve required to reintroduce control protocols during day phase: stasis fields restrict remaining major processing areas: limit virus capacity and reach: power reserves insufficient without direct sunlight: managed reduction required at nightfall—

"Wait, so you control the ship during the day? And the virus has it at night?"

—incorrect: excessive simplification—

"Fine – but something like that?"

—subjective assessment: correct—

"You've got a lot to learn about humans my friend," I mutter, before realising I'm still dictating for the display.

—correct— comes the reply.

It might be I only imagine that being said with a note of humour, but right now I'll take anything to distract me. Any spacer has a long list of things they're frightened of, but running out of air is on every list.

As is losing a crewmate and leaving them out in the great dark.

The terror threatens to overwhelm me when I focus on it, so I'll play imaginary word games with Ulu if necessary. Anything to turn my head from the looming void of fear that lingers on the edge of vision. The fear that an hour from now, I'm going to gasp and wheeze, claw at my helmet and scream my last. And then I'll slow, wind down like a toy and fall still, joining the spirits that haunt this wreck.

"Ghosts," I say suddenly, my panic prompting a memory. "You've been alone here for thousands of years – what was I seeing earlier? Did I imagine them?"

—projections: fragments drawn from ship records—

"Why?"

—threat assessment of unknown entity—

I laugh at that, hearing it tinged with faint hysteria and glad the dictation software doesn't describe it. "Me? You wanted to see if I was hostile? Just as well they almost gave me a heart-attack then!"

—illness yes/no—

"I..." I wave my hands, unable to give up such useless instinctive gestures even when they might confuse matters further. "An expression. Humorous, or meant to be anyway. The projections frightened me, made me want to run away."

—Understand: humorous—

There's a pause until I realise that's all they're saying on the subject and I have to hope I'm the butt of a joke. "Yeah, well... Do the star-thorns attack them?"

—movement induces assessment reaction: default hostile state—

That's all too easy to picture and I nod without speaking. Another thought worms its way into my head however, the memory of what Ulu had said earlier.

"Ship records? Didn't you say you burned the core system?"

—yes—

"The records were not kept there?"

There's a fractional hesitation, a twitch of the screen as

though Ulu had considered putting up one message in reply then replaced it.

—fragments retained elsewhere: personal communications: local memory: private storage—

“Those have survived?”

—estimate 0.01% of ship data survived attack uncorrupted: unknown quantity now degraded or infected—

“So you gathered the fragments?”

—preservation protocol commenced after 3000 day/night cycles: records salvaged during liminal period—

“Why? What changed? Do you have an imperative to preserve information?”

There’s a hesitation before a reply comes.

—Loss: outrage: defiance: fury: pride: love: grief—

The rapid succession of words leaves me stunned and silent for a while. Eventually I bow my head, unable to fully grasp a near-immortal sentient’s emotions as last survivor of a species-civilisation. I force myself to move on even though the words stick in my throat at first. There can be time for understanding later.

“And when you escape?” I ask in a small voice.

—fragments included in storage: histories of civilisation: art: technology: family—

“Your whole civilisation, contained in your head?” I gasp.

—no: insufficient capacity: additional storage required—

“Where?”

—provide directions: update plan of ship—

“You want me to go and fetch the records of your entire civilisation?”

—modification of escape vessel required: air supply limiting factor: survey drone status unknown—

I hesitate but only for a moment. If I were Ulu, fetching

those records would be my price for getting the fragile meat-sack interloper out too.

"Are you sure we can't leave it and come back? There are ships on their way."

—non-management of stasis fields: virus wins game: all remain sections of ship compromised—

"You could have just said 'no,' but point taken. I…"

Some part of me remains wary and with good reason. I don't know Ulu at all, nor their species or anything else. New AIs in our system go into the Playground, a sealed quarantine system where they can be assessed by their peers before release.

Or not. It's not something they discuss freely, so I've heard, but it's acknowledged some AIs don't leave. Destroyed or dumped into some contained network, it's never been clear. It could be a rumour they've permitted to make us humans feel safer for all I know. The only thing that could find an AI that doesn't want to be found is another AI. Humans wouldn't stand a chance.

The point is that it's a serious threat to planetary security to allow unknown AIs into an unrestricted system because of their mind-blowing capabilities. I'm trusting Ulu with my life, that's easy enough given my lack of options. Trusting them with my ship and a pipeline into the world my family live in, suddenly I'm not so sure.

—trust— Ulu says, perhaps interpreting my reticence.

"Can I?"

—necessary: both must trust—

"You want me to fetch the records of your civilisation."

—yes: trust: backup records low probability of non–corruption when game lost: 1 day/night cycle estimated before—

"I understand that," I interrupt, "but I don't know the records exist."

—understood: trickery/ruse yes/no?—

"You might be a threat to my planet, my civilisation. You might hold my family's lives while I hold your records."

—understood: unknown technological capacity: risk of integration with ship: offer of trust?—

"How do you mean?"

—survival unnecessary: ship remains in orbit after air supply zero yes/no?—

"Yes."

—survival becomes offer of trust: gesture—

"Of goodwill? Oh. Yes, I suppose so." I'm slightly stunned by that bald acknowledgement of my life's value, but I can't argue really. Ulu has a fair, albeit unpalatable, point.

Ulu reaches out a hand once more, but this time one finger blurs and loses cohesion. It's shape morphs grossly as I watch it, looking like some sort of hideous parasite. Of course it's probably not far different to the universal connector I'd used on the bay door when I tried to find a way out.

—trust?: update ship plan—

17

I hesitate so long it must seem to Ulu like I've had some sort of episode. Or I'm trying to decide between fight and flight. In all honestly, I don't know what to think. My brain shuts down briefly – bewildered, exhausted, grieving, and frightened, this is too much going on all in one little space for me to cope with. Turns out I'm not cut out to be a marine, however expensive my EVA suit was. Snap decisions, coolness under pressure. I feel none of that, just a yawning confusion that I don't know what in the dark I'm doing.

This being of another civilisation and another age wants me to trust them. This sentient AI I know nothing about. This machine with hopes, dreams, vast acres of grief, limbs that can snap me in two and – most likely – the processing capacity to put at least a serious dent in my home planet.

But what other option is there? Ulu could just as easily kill me and escape onto the *Sakakawea* afterwards. Am I any real impediment to them whatsoever? I don't know much about AIs, but I doubt it's worth their time trying to trick me. The *Sak's* computer won't prove a match for them either.

But still Ulu waits for me to catch up to their line of thinking – happy to let me come to a conclusion even if they've got one eye on my harpoon.

"Trust," I say at last and take a step forward, trying not to squirm at the sight of their hand turned worm-like.

Ulu bows their head fractionally, limbs lowering too, in a submissive gesture that I assume is acknowledgement or appreciation. Then they gently take my hand and the worms go to work. I don't feel it, they're not burrowing into flesh, but still it makes my skin crawl to watch.

A warning appears on my HUD, informing me of a system intrusion and doing the equivalent of screaming for help. I do nothing and soon it disappears, removed by Ulu as they go about their business. I've no doubt they're scanning my systems, checking out the layout and stored data, but all I see is the displayed image of the wreck shudder and twitch. Like a camera lens zooming in, one section becomes suddenly crisper, more detailed. Tiny starbursts of information flower on the projection, then it zooms in to show me the local area. A red dot appears and I realise it's me as it starts to move off – working through corridors and rooms until stopping abruptly.

'Records,' speaks a voice in my ear. 'Here.'

I flinch and barely manage not to shriek in alarm. The voice is calm and bland – not very different to the computer's own on my ship which I eventually realise is probably intentional.

'Ah, right then. And you?' I stammer.

The words appear on my projection still, but Ulu is looking right at me, using the internal system to speak more directly for as long as we're in physical contact.

'Escape vessel,' Ulu reminds me. 'Additional power required. Closed cargo hold. Isolated from power grid.'

'How do I find you?'

The projected map pulses, now highlighting a second path in green.

'Escape vessel. Estimate rendezvous.'

A point flashes up along the green route, about three-quarters along the route. Ulu is saying they are going to meet me on my way back and for some reason that gives me a sense of immediate relief.

Maybe the biologicals they were used to weren't so different to humans.

'How long?'

'Estimate, forty minutes.' The mission clock appears on my HUD. 'Preparation and launch, five minutes. flight to safe distance, forty minutes.'

'That doesn't leave us much time.'

'Correct.'

The red line appears on my HUD, a translucent arrow looking like it's being projected onto the floor. Ulu breaks off contact. All sound except my breathing vanishes. They look at me for a moment then turn and move swiftly away, vanishing into the darkness of the wreck.

'Right then,' I say to myself. 'Move quickly, Song. You don't have much air to play with.'

I walk as quickly as I can, faster than I had earlier. The thoroughfares of this wreck are at least laid out in a logical manner. So large a ship needs to be planned like a city built from scratch and I soon see familiar structures. A crossroad with vertical tubes at the centre. A chamber of the flower-like pods that I imagined as a nursery. This one is surrounded by a complex network of narrow side chambers, cramped spaces I don't investigate, the main room open on one side to a corridor as wide as a street.

It all makes me think of the builders as a more social

species than humans. The young free to mingle with passers-by. Family groups sharing a nest in their place of reverence, as I've decided the glowing trees are. Perhaps it's just a projection of my own hopes, but in this dark and cold place, it serves as a comfort all the same.

Ulu has left the mission clock on my HUD, whether by accident or design. As I see the minutes tick past, I start to move faster – more recklessly. Dangerous, I know, but I see it as a countdown to when I run out of air. I reactivate the motion-tracker then start to glide through rooms whenever I can. A check to investigate first of course, but the star-thorns are quicker than me – or at least unfettered by thought. The one that pursued caught up ground as much by blind fury as anything else, heedless of damage to itself.

Instead of creeping along, hoping I'll get away if I do encounter one, I'm trusting Ulu's plan. The game they've been playing for thousands of years – manoeuvring the physical pieces on the board or trapping them, denying their opponent the power it needs to effectively strategize. The red path remains constant, a reassuring presence instead of the ghostly overlay it really is.

I linger briefly at the bottom of a funnel-shaped room with sixty tiers rising up from a floor only five metres wide. A council chamber? The steep sides look perilous to a human, but I see three slopes with hand-holds rising all the way up and guess this species had no such concerns. Past that are grand offices of some sort – divided by fretwork walls that seem to depict foliage and thick glass screens, some opaque, others not. Many are badly damaged, a few choked with debris from shattered walls between them – hanging inert in the airless vacuum.

Unexpectedly, Ulu's route takes me around a corner and into an office-suite. It worms a path through successively smaller rooms until it brings me to a nondescript antechamber containing blockish storage units. One is highlighted on my HUD so I pull it open and inside there's exactly nothing. It's not easy to see all the way in when you're wearing an armoured space suit, but as best I can manage, there's really nothing there. I try some others and find only dust and fragments of whatever had been stored there.

There's no drawer directly below the highlighted one so after I've exhausted my options, I start to investigate it more closely. That whole row appears solid and unmoving, but it's simple enough to wrench the first drawer out and discover the cavity below. Inside is a cube with rounded corners, gunmetal grey like much of Ulu. It's decorated on every side, varying designs but all based around three circles, one within another and all touching at the same point. There's a recessed handle on the top of the cube so it's simple enough for me to pull out and hold it up for inspection.

It's bulky and feels solid. Weight means nothing in zero-g of course, but mass remains. It's not quite like hefting a solid block of steel, but very unwieldy all the same. Not just the usual gel-racks of the *Sak's* memory storage, this feels more rigid and dense. I spend a while inspecting it, leaving the thing to hover and slowly spin, but aside from decoration there's little to see. The gold circles are indented slightly and I wonder if the variation serves as multiple connectors.

Speculation gets me nowhere however and almost immediately I'm nagged into setting off again. My HUD pulses once before the red overlay vanishes. It's replaced with a green indicator leading me back the way I'd come. I feel a vague sense of disappointment, like I should have earned some sort of reward for completing the quest, but the mission clock keeps on ticking by.

I take the cube by the handle and start off, then shift to cradling it in both arms. The EVA suit is more than strong enough to deal with the mass, but it's too bulky to be comfortable at my side when gliding isn't an option. Once settled, I resume my brisk pace, trying to shave precious minutes off Ulu's estimate. The green path is a comforting source of focus. With my attention on it I spend less time looking at my surroundings, limiting that to an assessment of every new stretch.

I need to stay safe, but the mission clock preys on my mind all the while. The green path keeps me steady. Keeps my mind off the emptiness and shifting darkness, the remains of the dead and danger that swims through it.

My path quickly deviates. I follow a crawl-tube up, heading for the hull according to my new map. It brings me past several levels, the uppermost of which has a more militaristic feel to the design. I see one broken nest-tree, dark and tilted with one of the base trunks shattered entirely. Above that is my destination and I crawl cautiously out into a chamber with a low ceiling, helmet lights showing a forest of ceramic-like growths. At the base of each are trenches filled with hard-frozen dirt – a fair amount of debris hanging above them too.

I pick a slow path through it all, unable to avoid speculating on the lives that might have been there once. Soon it brings me out into a huge domed space bigger than any I've seen up to that point and I stop dead, stunned by the sight. It's easily two hundred metres across with a – in ship terms – colossal empty space beneath the high dome.

Checking the map again I realise this is just a smaller version of the big domes we'd spotted from the outside, towards the front of the wreck. I'm not afforded a view of the stars as I'd hoped, but it's still beautiful in its own sad way. Paths lead around a variety of structures that dot the ground – there are flat open spaces and shallow pond-like bowls.

Here, more than any part I've seen, was a community place – not just offices, workshops, homes, or even temples. No, here they lived and played. Fell in love perhaps or basked in the delight of their offspring running free. It humbles me as much as it tugs at my heart, spurring me on to get home at any cost.

Around the outside there are a variety of tree-facsimiles, none glowing or as grand as the temple ones. Many are draped in what must have been ropes or some other organic material, meaning I have to choose my path carefully. I start out across it then hesitate, feeling vulnerable in such an open space. After a while my courage returns and I continue, taking an oblique path that keeps me close to cover at all times.

Only when I'm on the other side and entering the ring of trees do I let the tension flow out of me a little. It doesn't last long. As I enter the open gallery beyond my motion tracker starts to ping once again.

18

I drop behind the nearest obstacle and switch off my lights, heart hammering.

It's Ulu coming to check up on me, right? It has to be.

I don't know if I'm reassuring myself or bargaining with the universe, but whatever I'm doing, I'm doing it without moving. That memory has overridden anything else, Ulu's words about the star-thorns.

Movement. Movement attracts their attention.

The suit helps me there. While the person inside is panting, biting her lip, shivering with terror, the tin can around this fleshy feast is unmoved. The sensors aren't so sensitive to transmit every little twitch into servo-action. As soon as I've squatted down as best the suit allows, cube resting on my toes, I'm just an inert lump of metal.

Pleasingly shaped metal no doubt, I think, trying to distract myself from the fear, *but I doubt mindless kills-units will have much appreciation for the female form.*

For a while I see nothing. The gallery is long and deep, smashed at one end with a bewildering array of explosive- and heat- damage that's turned it into a climbing frame of twisted metal. Finally I see it, crawling heavily from beneath that mess. A star-thorn for certain, but unlike the others I've seen. This one's massive, comfortably bigger than my shuttle, with three main whip-arms manoeuvring it awkwardly through the tangle.

It's impossible to make out anything. The star-speckled night sky of its skin eludes comprehension. Without my lamps I feel all the colder and more lost out there, but there's a stasis field behind it that gives some sense of a silhouette.

My mind guesses at four pulsing, faintly curved kite shapes that meet at one end. A broad arm, crooked and studded with fat thorns, rises from the centre of each except one where there's perhaps a stub. Damage or some other tool, I can't say. Each one is surrounded by lesser arms, some maybe even growing off the main branch? I can't see well enough to be sure, but still feel all the creeping repulsiveness I normally reserve for oil spiders – just on a vast scale.

It heaves itself forward until it's at the edge of the damaged area, stretching forward a long limb that looks like a tentacle built out of obsidian. The surface isn't entirely a light-drinking black, however. I half-see ragged shapes and lines on it too. Nothing definite, not in this blackness, but gives it a corpse-like air. Jutting bone and torn flesh. With a jerk it propels forward, as silent as a ghost, and I barely see it glide lazily past my hiding spot.

I fight the urge to scream. It's no more than fifteen metres away and passing out of my field of vision. I can't turn. I can't do anything more than sit and wait and hope. It's all too easy to imagine the flash of jagged thorns, the monstrous embrace. The pressure and the tearing. The wheeze of leaking air and pain of slicing.

I watch the motion tracker, that imperfect after-thought

of tech giving dull blips to indicate position. My teeth are gritted so tight it hurts, blood pounding hard enough I start to worry the star-thorn might feel the vibrations through the floor. But I don't move. I don't run. I don't shudder or faint for all I feel like I'm going to. I don't cover my mouth with my hand to smother the urge to scream.

I. Don't. Move. A. Muscle.

And slowly it drifts away. The pulse of the motion tracker grows fainter. The numbers beneath it increase. But it's still there, somewhere in the open ground while the signal starts to wobble as the tree-shapes interfere with it. Can I trust the numbers? Can I move without it seeing? Can I risk staying? It might be patrolling this whole open space on a set loop, I've no way of knowing. Surely not, I think, if Ulu sent me this way, but how long should I take the risk?

It's forty-eight metres away when the signal drops out. It was wavering badly in the last few so I don't think it's just stopped moving. The machine's progress was steady, moving from fixed point to fixed point in an unhurried fashion. It's probably just out of range, screened by the trees. I turn my head ever so slightly to follow the unchanging green line Ulu has laid for me, breadcrumbs through the forest. The way looks clear and the motion tracker doesn't ping again.

I rise and look behind me. I can't see it. It's so dark without my lights I can barely see a thing, but I know it would be suicide to turn them on. All I can do is prime the manoeuvring jets in case I need to flee.

Don't waste time, I tell myself. *Just get out of here without tripping over yourself.*

I almost laugh at that. The automatic fear of making a noise, of attracting attention. In a vacuum.

It's the fall that'll kill you, not the landing, I add, hysteria running free through my mind. One last look then I turn to my path once more. Picking my steps, moving clear of my hiding place, setting my sights on an archway exit. One foot after the other, the reassuring clunk of boots getting a good contact with the floor, the pant of my breath loud in my ears once again.

It's slow going without the lights. I can't hurry, can't move as fast as I had before. The stasis field is all the light I have to work with despite the suit enhancing as best it can. It illuminates so little I kick piece after piece of debris, sending them spinning away through the gloom. One even slams into the stasis field, jerked to a gloopy halt and pinned like a butterfly in the books of old.

Once I'm past halfway, the motion tracker starts to shriek. I glance back and scream too. It's there! Somehow it's spotted me and is hauling its way forward as fast as those huge tentacles can reach. Another few steps and I'd have not noticed it in time, but the thing's damaged, favouring the side with only one arm.

I slam on the jets as I'd been taught when I first took up wreck-diving – emergency action. They never expected anything like this, but debris is a very real threat. The memory cube drags at me as I dart forward, aiming for the arch. I sense as much as see the dark mass fly past, one tentacle whipping out and clipping my shoulder plate.

It spins me but the suit gyroscopes compensate, pull me back on track before I can see through the panic. I'm past praying at that point, adrenalin pumping, training at work through the chaos in my mind. There's no human inside the suit now, just a primitive ancestor fleeing a predator. All fear and desperation. But I make it to the arch without being torn apart, without alarms screaming that my suit's losing pressure.

I'm no expert with the jets, but manage to turn the corner without smashing into it. I keep going, screaming for the suit to activate lights and find myself in a high alley-type corridor. Certainly large enough to fly down. I just need to leave what's beyond it for future-me to worry about. As it is, I'm in a frantic scramble for the other end, barely managing to correct my flight before I bounce from one wall to the other.

I can't look back, not like this, but the motion tracker gives me all the warning I need. I'm about halfway to the far door before it pings again to tell me the star-thorn is in sight once again. I go high, describing an awkward arc back down to the doorway again. With luck it'll aim high as it pushes off. Worth a try I hope. No time to second guess – down I go. Through the door I'm blinded by the brightness of my own lamps on silver walls, metal polished to a mirror shine. There's a long tube running most of the length of the room.

Easily large enough to walk along, it has a scattering of green lights winking around its edge. I'm plunging for it but I'm not going to make it around the glittering frame of lights. Fear of any active computer system is overridden by the more immediate terror of cracking my helmet on the edge. Awkwardly I readjust, catching one edge with the memory cube but missing my head by centimetres. The momentum takes me down to the nominal floor and I feel the impact through my legs before it drags me into the tube.

Inside it's featureless – white panels edged with gold. The tube blazes bright under my lights as I lurch onward, spinning around to get a brief view of the thing chasing me.

The nightmare's already at the entrance, just a dozen metres behind. This time the suit can't compensate and I just carry on down the tube, a lighthouse all of my own while darkness comes ever onward. Before I know it, I'm out the other side. One final impact against the side arrests my spin enough for the suit to stabilise me. I slam on the jets to push up, but even as I do so there's a shudder and pulse of light. A blue glow cracks through my vision, distorting the frantic motion tracker, and then I'm up and out of the way.

Despite my best efforts, I thump heavily into the ceiling. There I manage to stay, anchored by a hand-hold I grab before I can float away. I swing around it, momentum refusing to be denied and have to twist to avoid smashing the memory cube against the metal ceiling, letting my shoulder-plate take the blow instead.

Finally I stop, panting, as the tip of one obsidian-blade tentacle drifts forward out of the tube. I wail, unable to hold the terror in but even as I do so the tentacle crosses to the wall, thumping silently against it. It's detached. Cut away by the stasis field inside whatever that tube is. I don't know how or why there are so many such fields throughout the ship – presumably it's a repurposed tech or something for long-distance travel. Right now I don't care, I'm just pathetically grateful they're rigged to trap the star-thorns.

Before my heart's stopped pounding, before I can breathe without gulping in terror, a wall panel opens. Ulu half-emerges and follows the beam of my lights up until they've found me. When they do, they give me an oddly formal and clipped wave. Before I can even think about responding, the wall panel lights up with a word.

—concern—

At that, I burst out laughing. Or crying. Probably both.

19

Eventually I control myself and push down to the floor. Once my boots lock on, I start to feel calmer, anchored in both senses. Part of me doesn't want to investigate the tube but I force myself and feel my skin crawl at the sight within. The tattered star-thorn fills most of the space within, amorphous and seemingly without depth as the light fails to fully describe its proportions. Tentacles reach forward for purchase or for prey and the sight reminds me to check my shoulder plate.

The metal is scored deep. I dare not touch it for fear of snagging something on the sharp edge, but somehow those great thorns – even in passing – have cut right into metal. Only the thickness of the armour saved me from a serious injury. I'd probably be alive – I have filler to patch holes in the suit – but what that would have done to flesh is anyone's guess. Even ignoring the effects of cold and pressure loss.

—injured?— the wall asks on Ulu's behalf.

I shake my head as I activate the text log to reply.

"No. Almost though. This ah... this isn't where we were meant to meet. Is there a problem?"

—unusual activity: unable to access cargo hold—

"What? We can't get out? I thought you had the virus contained?"

—previous yes: circumstance has changed: uncertain effect but external influence likely—

"External... wait, what?" I gasp. "You mean me? You think I've done something?"

—game of night and day— comes the gnomic reply. —all factors predicted/controlled/balanced: unusual activity among star-thorns: patrol patterns altered: search initiated—

"I don't understand."

—increased coordination: power consumption by major virus hubs unchanged: unknown factor—

"How could I do anything? I... I didn't bring..."

I can't finish the sentence. I realise I did exactly that – brought additional power onto the ship. Not much, not anything that would matter in normal circumstances, but the shuttle's computers and engines are powered by the same source. A source that I hooked up to the bay door when I was trying to open up again...

"My shuttle," I admit in a quiet voice, shocked and ashamed by my unintended actions.

—virus moving to active search: analysis of entry point: known power capacity of shuttle?—

"Do I know the...?" I shake my head. "No, sorry."

—escape procedure rendered inoperable: alternative method required—

"Alternative? No! There's no time! My air, it'll run out. We can't come up with another plan, it's impossible."

—route impassable: multiple units on active search pattern—

I don't say anything. For a few moments my mind is

entirely blank, stunned by the looming idea that I could be about to die. Could watch the minutes count down almost to the very moment of my death. Just time enough for one last message to my family in the hope that any salvage team has better luck that I do.

I imagine it will. For a prize like this, the company will make the effort. The first team might all die if I can't tell them about the star-thorns, the virus, but they'll work it out. A few dozen dead compared to colossal profits? They'll work it out – go low tech and wipe out the physical threat, isolate the ethereal one and render it harmless. Then they'll pass my message on. Perhaps. In a few years, maybe, depending on what it says.

I need to word it carefully, I realise, feeling light-headed. *If there's nothing that needs to be censored, the company will release it. Tell them there was an accident, or some sort of cover story. If I absolve the company of any culpability they might even compens—*

I stop. I'm not dead yet. Now's not the time for these thoughts. I check the mission clock and air reserve. It's not an exact measurement, but it gives me an approximate idea of how long I have left to live. And I do want to live, I really bloody do. I want to see my family again and I'd rather die trying than just wait – watching the sands run out.

There's a fraction under an hour left. It's enough, but not if we don't have a way to get off the ship. We need that escape route – no, *I* need it. Ulu can stay here another thousand years without needing a whole lot. I just have to hope they're not keen on the prospect.

"I have an idea. It's... risky."

—high probability of death— Ulu replies.

"Hey, at least wait until I tell you my plan!"

—all assessed contingencies exceed 50% probability—

"How about getting off the ship? I don't care about how much air I've got afterwards – I trust my people. Can we get off the ship?"

—yes: continued high probability of death—

I hesitate. I don't know if it's even fair to try and persuade Ulu to attempt it. Synthetics have their compulsions they can't always overcome the way humans can face a fear or control a phobia. Ulu was made part of this ship from what I can tell, but they're alive and sentient. I can't push too hard without asking.

"Are you hard-wired to obey living creatures?"

—no—

"Are you, um, required to preserve life of crew or residents on this ship? Or other sentient life of any kind?"

—no—

"So if I ask for your help, you're not obliged to do whatever you can to keep me alive?"

—no—

"Okay, good."

—unexpected response—

That throws me, but I guess it is. Sien Nau wrestled with the question for several hundred years. We weren't the ones to pay the highest price for enslavement of sentient systems, but we had to take a damn hard look at ourselves afterwards.

Plenty of people left for other planets when it became clear AIs were driving the conversation, but plenty more listened. Plenty agreed or were persuaded and as the generations moved on, our thinking adjusted to accept the new, prosperous world we lived in.

"Like I said, I've got a plan, but it's risky for us both. It's not as much of a risk for me because I'm dead if I don't get off this ship soon. But for you, there's no rush. Others will come. I don't know how they will react to you, but unless you claim ownership over this ship, they'll treat you fairly I expect."

—ownership: unnecessary—

Ulu reached out and gently plucked the memory cube from my hands.

—sufficient—

"Then they'll probably let you live and value you, even, given you know more about this ship than they could discover in a hundred years."

—worth understood: request for assistance remains?—

I duck my head, almost ashamed. Not about pleading for my life – I'll do that in a heartbeat if it'll do any good, but something tells me Ulu is making their own mind up.

"Yes," I say at last. "I would like your help. I would like to live."

—acknowledged— there's a pause, long enough that I imagine a vast calculation going on. —weapon required— Ulu says eventually.

"I... what?" for a moment my mind is blank but then I consider what I had been going to suggest. "Yes – a weapon or explosive. Several if you have them."

—come—

20

We move quickly. The seconds and minutes are ticking by faster and faster, so it feels to me. Ulu needs no chivvying along though. I'm moving as quick as I can and they match my urgency perfectly – another calculation no doubt. We can't talk, not when we're moving that way, and the frustration bubbles up inside me. I want to talk through the plan but there's no time to stop, no time to waste.

I have to trust Ulu – trust this alien AI I've barely had a full conversation with, let alone found reason to trust. Because there's nothing else to do, no sensible decision that isn't based on faith. And I'm dead anyway in less than an hour. It could easily be the case that Ulu can see no viable way for me to survive whatever we try and is going to expend me as a resource. The thought keeps rattling around my head, but I find a sort of peace in it. I'm going to die anyway, why not in the service of keeping another sentient being alive? Better than pointlessly, right? Small consolation, but enough.

By fits and starts, I search for a voice recorder in the suit computer while Ulu takes us on a small diversion. I consider turning off my screen in the interests of privacy, but don't. Ulu has three hundred and sixty degree vision. Anything suspicious might cause them to make a change to the plan, to doubt my motives. More than anything though, I don't want to doubt *them*. The slender hope of survival is all that's keeping me sane and Ulu's honesty is the foundation of that. Imagined or otherwise, to dwell on the alternative brings a physical pain. A pulse behind my eyes I can't allow if I'm to stand any chance.

If these are my last moments, I don't want them to be wasted on mistrust.

From inside the broken guts that spill from a smashed machine, Ulu removes a trio of blockish objects the length of my arm. They're clearly made to fit snugly into a hand – or one the shape of Ulu's at least. It's less comfortable for me when they pass me the other, but with a little awkwardness I manage to hold it in a similar fashion.

With all the brisk gentleness of a parent, Ulu unpicks my hand from the weapon and points out the dangerous parts – illustrating the effects on a wall panel and cautioning me from squeezing the part I'd grabbed it by. It's a short-range weapon that spreads and diffuses its effects, no doubt designed especially on board a ship where you don't want anything punching too far forward. Whether it still works or not I've no idea, but I keep the dangerous end pointing away from my companion and plod on, hoping it's no more than a precaution.

I record a short message for my family as we move off again. There's no time for anything else and what really can I say? I just need to tell them I love them one more time – as though I could ever say it enough. Life's taught me that much at least and I'm reminded of my grandfather's favourite saying:

"Be sparing with your anger, quiet with your hate and neither with your love."

I can only whisper it across the vast reaches of space, but I hope that will be enough.

I finish just as Ulu stops and I realise we're at our first destination. It's a tall room with ten identical tiers on either side of a narrow space. What look like complex workstations occupy regular intervals on each tier. Several are illuminated by stasis fields – two contain light-eluding nightmares, the third is empty but blast damage at the rear has opened a path to some adjoining space. All part of Ulu's great game I imagine, denying ground to the enemy.

I stand holding the memory cube, my only value here being a handy place to put stuff. The weapon I don't understand of course, but it's not difficult to work out what Ulu intends. They set it right at the edge of the nearer stasis field, lock it into a complicated array of spidery appendages then melt one finger into an interface panel. Ulu is still for just a few seconds before withdrawing and shunting the array forward so the furthest part of the weapon is pressed into the stasis field.

That done they turn away, collect the cube once more and perform the same elegant scooping gesture of asking me to follow. I do so – this time pressed just to keep up while Ulu moves with the effortless grace of a thousand years of practice. Gliding from place to place, reaching for alternating hand-holds as though performing a dance, it's mesmeric even as I lumber along trying to keep up. I use my jets liberally in the large spaces, trusting Ulu to know it's safe despite the increased activity. More weird and wonderful places stream past me, half-seen and mostly ignored. Spherical chambers like angular bubbles packed together, communal spaces so filled with floating wreckage we dare not enter. One long shaft where I see lights flickering in the distance – the virus working around whatever limits or controls Ulu has managed to establish during the day.

It hurts my head to consider – the thousands of years in an unwinnable struggle, increasingly futile as the chances of either civilisation surviving dwindles. There must be other relics of both, presumably far beyond the reaches of human-discovered space, but right now this wreck contains all that remains of either in any tangible form.

I block it all out. The wonder and the tragedy both. For me there's only light and shadow, Ulu and my mission clock. It's not long before we arrive at a nondescript service corridor where control channels and pipes fill each wall. There Ulu stops and hands me the cube before retrieving a blockish object, as long as my arm and with one rounded end. They make a gesture I don't understand. They make it again then reach out to the control channel, causing a section of the wall above it to be marked with words.

—extinguish lights—

I balk at the suggestion. Without them I'm blind, close to useless. The suit's HUD can enhance available light, but nothing more without the motion tracker pinging away. With the wreck still in shadow, there won't be enough for it to work with.

"How do I see?"

—Ulu guide: star-thorns track light: alternate illumination pending—

"I can't be any use in the dark!"

—carrying majority of remaining knowledge and art of a civilisation—

"Sure, if you put it like that, but so could a donkey."

—pending: negative: incompatible with suit—

Somehow I laugh at that. Either Ulu's miserably literal or their sense of humour isn't so different to my own. Switching out the lights I keep my gun in one hand, the cube in the other. As soon as I do so, I have to fight the urge to bring the lights back up. I can't see a damned thing and my panic response kicks in, using my air up even faster which stresses me further. Without the light I'm entirely vulnerable, deep in the belly of the whale and feeling the pressure of darkness driving in on all sides.

I feel a slight pressure on my arm and realise Ulu is accessing my computer again. It takes a little while for me to work out why but then a red indicator appears on my HUD, a simplified version of Ulu's shape. It vanishes when they stop moving but reappears just as quickly and I realise they've tweaked the motion detector to follow them.

So I can't see where I'm going? Just blindly follow them? Sounds like fun. Definitely not bait for those damn star-thorns – nope, not at all.

My mission clock is ticking away all the time and it's enough to send a spike of anxiety through my gut. The warning indicators are red, flashing at the corner of my vision. Other than distracting me, they're not doing any bloody good so I get the suit to override them. I think I've got the point by now. All the same, without them I feel even more swallowed by darkness.

'Activating diversion,' I hear inside my helmet.

It's a relief to hear that flat computer voice again, even if there's no accompanying words on a panel.

'What about...?' I begin, as much to test my own text display. Nothing comes up and I realise Ulu's remembered to shut that down as well. I feel lost without it now, angry that they've done that without telling me and left me lacking even the faint glow to see by. It takes a great will of effort to push that aside, but that's what I need to do.

'Contact will be lost,' Ulu informs me. 'No further instructions possible. Follow red light. Ignore walls.'

'Ignore walls?'

'Terrain will reshape on set path until virus countermeasure. Follow red light. Remain within four metres.'

'And then we're out?'

They indicate the object they've collected. 'Propulsion reconfiguration required. Escape vessel checks. Exit activation. Virus will reassert control before exit. High probability need to defend position.'

'I'm no soldier,' I warn.

'Acknowledged. Limited range of weapon, maximum ten metres distance to arrest momentum. Significant damage to star-thorns only within three metres.'

'I keep them off while you work – I can do that.' Being given a job cheers me, even if it's a last resort – anything not to be dead weight right now.

'Acknowledged. Counting down. 3 – 2 – 1 – activating diversion.'

21

I can't tell if anything has happened, let alone whether it's gone to plan. Yet more trust piled on top of the rest, but Ulu is content to assume it's worked. Or knows for certain perhaps. I've still no real handle on what level of access they have through an interface panel, but surely the stasis field network will give enough of a clue. How long we need to wait is a trickier prospect. If there are patrols close, the destruction of one should send them on a war footing – more alert but hopefully converging on where the other was destroyed.

Unless some idiot gave the virus enough power to properly assess things and recognise a diversion.

If that's true, there's nothing I can do about it. There's no time for a plan B, just blind faith in plan A. Ulu remains still and invisible to me for a good twenty seconds, frozen in the act of movement. Long enough that I wonder if they've had some sort of systems failure, the virus has finally torn into their central processor, or they've simply given up and are waiting for me to run out of air.

Finally Ulu moves, a blur of red across my HUD. Only

movement registers, everything else is still too dark for my HUD to enhance/extrapolate. An arm, then a hand, before everything falls black for a second. Then I jump at the sight of Ulu wrenching off a panel from the wall. An entire section of metal, lifted away with superhuman strength and tossed aside. They move into the gap and I watch in astonishment until they're almost gone from view and remember I must keep close behind.

I stumble forward, burdened by cube and gun, just making it through the gap in time to see a wall in the small adjoining room fold neatly down. The red light that accompanies the movement is dull, less bright than the outline of Ulu moving into the revealed space. I tramp onwards, trying to get as close as I can without tripping them. More walls fall away. It's some sort of storage space, adaptable to requirements and right now we need a clear path.

Ulu presses forward, one wall half-dropping ahead of us before whipping back up. I only glimpse movement within but I assume it's a star-thorn, unexpectedly left behind or trapped by these shifting walls. We move on, almost running along an oblique path now as walls drop in front of Ulu and close up behind me. The first stutter of light overhead makes me cringe – like lightning heralding a monster's reanimation. Ulu falters and changes direction, setting off on a new path now as though it was always part of the plan.

Another star-thorn is revealed and this one lashes a barbed tentacle towards Ulu. Before it strikes, the avatar has their gun up. A silent, blurred detonation slaps it back again. I see only what my HUD can translate, but I think fragments are flying even as the wall returns. There's no time to ask, no time to doubt. We press on. Our lives depend on that.

Wall after wall vanishes. I imagine them thudding into

place behind me, but I hear nothing. Once I check to watch it happen, but I know I can't linger. The reassurance has to be imagined, embraced as an article of faith because otherwise there's just shadows and tentacles. I feel no vibrations through my feet, just the hasty *thunk* of my boots locking to the floor. We twist and turn, now taking an arcing path that reveals glimpses of heavy machinery, lashed down, stored tight.

More stutters of light come and Ulu slams to a halt against a wall that's not opened – one hand pressed flat against it. I realise then there must be an interface there. Ulu clearly doesn't have remote access to the ship so they must be manually switching between pre-programmed cascade patterns. No doubt as the virus attacks whatever defences Ulu has built, it switches to a new track, but the discovery of star-thorns might require direct intervention.

Sure enough the wall to their right folds down and Ulu storms through the gap. The light's coming faster now though and while it gives me more glimpses of my surroundings, my heart slams against my chest as I fear the implications. How far we've gone I've no idea. We've passed through dozens of spaces now – more than I've managed to count.

Still we keep on moving through identical units – occasionally having to squeeze our way around or over dark crates. The flashes of light help me there, give me a sense of what I'm flapping at so I can plan a path, but only a hint. More than once I slam into something unseen or the blur of Ulu's arm across my face brings me up short just in time. Then we're off again, our path taking increasingly abrupt changes of direction.

Finally Ulu stops at one lashed-down machine no different to the rest from what I can tell in the glimpses I receive. They rip away the covering for this one and I see it's the skeleton frame of some sort of drone. It's little more than a sledge with a drive unit at the rear and a halo frame around it bearing directional jets, but I'll take anything right now. Ulu leans over it and starts checking components – physically checking I realise rather than interfacing with a computer.

This sled is analogue, perhaps except for whatever is powering it but even that looks cobbled-together if not built from scratch. They slot the additional unit into the central space and start to link it up. Down the sides of that are long compartments, round-nosed and looking like missiles. I don't think they're weapons though, just equipment. Ulu won't be planning on returning any time soon.

There are cables and mismatched shapes neatly bound by metal bands, looking like organised junk until lights on the drive engine flicker into life. The fractured light gives an imperfect view of what's I'm trusting my life to, but given the state of it that's probably a good thing.

With brisk blurred movements Ulu checks over each part – ensuring everything remains intact and in working order. I look around, trying to figure out where we're getting out through the hull. Even as I do so the facing wall folds down to reveal a great cliff of vertical panels that must be the outer hull. There's no clear exit but a large ring has been placed on the inside of the nearest.

It looks thin, too small to be an iris doorway or anything, but even as I watch Ulu takes a narrow object from inside the sled and tosses it towards the ring. It sails over and locks onto the hull just as red lights burst into life all around the ring. Those flash a few times then the entire frame explodes into light – searingly bright and fierce enough to melt a hole right the way through.

A small silent explosion detonates a few seconds later, the thrown object I realise, sending the excised disc spinning away into the great dark. The glitter of starlight through the hole in the hull is the most beautiful thing I've seen but I can't stop to admire it. While I gape the room abruptly illuminates, a pale green glow appearing from somewhere above.

Then, as one, all of the walls fall away.

I blink in the weak light, struggling to comprehend what I'm seeing immediately. The room is huge, far bigger than I'd imagined. It runs for several hundred metres in three directions, a good forty high. Out of the corner of my eye I see Ulu kick away something tethering the sled, but that's not what grabs my attention.

There are black tangles spread all around the huge cargo hold – a dozen or more and all turning our way. Ulu darts across the sled, removing a cable while at the same time bringing their weapon to bear.

I glance over and yelp at the thrashing black mess of a star-thorn just five metres away. All I can make out is a confusion of red movement-tracking and reality, but something strikes the star-thorn and slaps it backwards. I don't see any damage, but nor anything for it to catch hold of and arrest its movement. The nightmare spirals away towards the outer wall, but more are closing in.

I drop the memory cube into the sled and stand ready to either leap in at Ulu's command or repel boarders. A smaller star-thorn is gliding forward towards us, tentacles spread wide ready to envelop me. Once moving it can't stop or change direction so I let it get almost as close as Ulu had before firing. The weapon jolts my arm, but the suit is more than capable of handling it. I see one tentacle torn away, the rest of the machine spun backwards into the path of another closing fast.

Ulu fires at one more, counteracting its momentum so the thing hangs rather comically in the air, before they get into the sled. I do the same, but there are more closing. I have to shoot twice before I can repel the nearest massive horror. At the back of my mind I feel the realisation that it won't last – the virus will find a way to compensate, there are too many for us to fight off at once, but this is all I've got.

Then I look around and realise we won't get moving in time. The rest are closing from their far positions, streaming in on all sides. I realise I'm dead. We're dead. There's no getting out of this. The sled's still not moving and Ulu is reaching past me to do something with the power unit, but unless it's got savage acceleration I don't see how we're making it.

And then a miracle happens. The ghosts of the wreck rise to our defence.

22

I'm too startled to move. Like an army they come, surging up from the ground to form a protective phalanx around us. They don't hold the line however, too hungry for revenge against the machines that killed them all those years ago.

Everything becomes a chaotic blur of movement. Even with the steady background lighting of the cargo hold, the elemental forces defy understanding. The star-thorns as elusive as the far reaches of space, hiding texture and shape, while the ghosts are insubstantial wisps that spin and surge restlessly. Six limbs like Ulu, but all sizes and shapes. At the heart of each is a red streak like the blood of their death wounds.

They rise and are magnificent – fearless in their assault. Cohorts sweep left and right, swirl around the furious thrashing of their enemy. Unfettered by momentum they split and move, never stopping for a moment. Each sweep confuses and distracts as hundreds move through seamlessly choreographed complexity. But they are ghosts, I remind myself, projections from Ulu's own memory. They cannot harm the nightmares; they only win us precious moments.

Even as I think it the first explosion winks in the gloom – then another and another, then firecracker bursts of fury. With a shock I see one star-thorn drift close to us, its nightmare skin shuddering under a volley of small explosions. I use my gun to drive it away, hoping to exploit whatever damage it's sustaining.

I glance at Ulu, still tinkering with the sled – working to fix something it appears. Their plans have been longer in the preparation than I realise, seeding the cargo hold somehow with miniature drones. A fitting use for those memories, I realise, each one loaded onto some sort of light projector along with an explosive charge.

That's what my adapted motion sensor is seeing as red-streaks. But the star-thorns are heedless. Not only can they shrug off a terrible battering, they don't seem to care. Dozens of impacts erupt together and the things continue to move, to fight. They draw closer, swatting at the ghosts flitting between them and their prey. We're running out of time I want to shout, but all I can do is hold my ground.

Ulu slips gracefully out of the sled, moving round to the propulsion block at the rear. I cannot even guess at how it works; I'm no use here. All I can do is stand and shoot at another star-thorn, this one closing with intent, but it brushes off the impact. Ulu fires too, smaller limbs still working on the propulsion block, and knocks it back a little further as the ghosts swarm in and lend their weight to the attack.

It isn't dissuaded and pushes forward again, but even as it does so the sled shudders. It rises a short way then stops – tethered by something underneath. Ulu fires once more then pulls themself back in, dropping the weapon in the process and placing one hand onto the memory cube. They beckon me inside and point to their feet, extending through the sled's skeleton frame to lock onto the floor beneath.

Without understanding I do the same. My boots latch to the nominal floor and on instinct I grab the sled with my free hand, bracing myself. The star-thorn closes, five metres, four. Its spines lash out but then there's a great kick from beneath. It's like a giant has just grabbed the entire cargo hold and jerked it upwards.

Everything moves – hurled away into the ceiling like the world's been flipped upside down. I see the star-thorns crash heavily into the ridged metal above. Some burst, metal frame skeletons jutting like bones through bloodless flesh. My stomach is almost hauled out through my mouth. For a moment I'm hanging upside down, too shocked and pained to appreciate what's happening, but then it's gone. The force fades almost as quickly as it's come and my weight disappears.

Gravity, or whatever inversion of it Ulu activated, releases the star-thorns but we're already moving. I can feel a faint vibration through the sled frame as the power unit builds and pushes us towards the aperture. I'm still looking up as a rain of nightmares starts to descend – stooping from all parts of the cargo hold. There's one almost directly above us. Its tentacles lash as it glides closer, but the sled slips past a second before it reaches us. For an instant I think we're free then a long barbed arm swings across me. My raised gun takes the worst of the impact. It slams against my shoulder and I feel something buckle, but I'm hunched down in the sled and the blow glances over my ducked head.

Ulu isn't so lucky, upright at the controls. The great black arm catches them squarely and tips them sideways.

They're shoved up and out of the rough framework as the arm snags on the lattice halo of the manoeuvring jets. I see that warp, crumpling partly before the tentacle drags free. Ulu tumbles, one hand still gripping the memory cube, but as they spin away they manage to lock onto the floor with one hand.

Gun held in their middle limbs, Ulu twists and fires, once, twice. I see the impact tear strips of darkness from the nightmare, driving it briefly off, but then I'm past. Unguided the sled continues moving for the opening in the hull, headed for the stars beyond. I flail briefly, but Ulu's beyond my reach and I'm still going – facing back in shock and astonishment as Ulu watches me.

Star-thorns close on all sides, a rising tide of darkness that the few remaining ghosts can only slow. In two seconds I'm at the hole, barely avoiding the edge, accelerating and almost free. I try to work my way up to the controls to swing it around. The buckled ring of metal hampers me though. I can't push past it and I'm getting further and further away. I howl, turning back towards Ulu who is running after me, still firing at the converging star-thorns. The avatar doesn't stand a chance, in seconds they'll be overwhelmed, and I just sit there aghast as I leave them behind.

My gun is gone, I can't turn the sled around. All I have is... my harpoon! I don't think, there's no time. I straighten my arm and yell for the suit to fire it. At first nothing happens. The wall of darkness has almost overwhelmed Ulu then there's a kick and a flash of movement. The bolt slams out so fast I can hardly see it against the chaos. If Ulu sees it coming, they don't have time to move or react. No doubt trajectories are calculated, damage assessed, contingencies planned, all in the blink of an eye.

The bolt strikes home and lodges, bursting savagely

through metal. I see Ulu jolted by the impact, staggered, and spun half-around, while the star-thorns reach for their prey – so long denied to them.

'Lock!' I shriek, jabbing the manual buttons at the same time. 'Recall!'

Slowly it responds, or so it seems to me, but respond it does. The micro-cable, rapidly unspooling as the sled drags me away, locks and holds. I see it pull taut as the sled's speed increases and I draw further from the great cliff of the wreck's hull. Just as the first tentacle is about to envelop Ulu they're yanked out of reach, towards the hull breach. The memory cube comes first and finally I see that's what I hit, not Ulu's body at all but the precious repository of their entire civilisation.

There's no time to mourn it, no time to wonder what might be salvaged. I see Ulu dragged away as arms of night slash inward. Plucked from the very heart of them, Ulu is buffeted and scraped by the thorns but snared by nothing and then they're out. Clear of the ship that's been their tomb for more than a hundred thousand years. Clear of the unrelenting hunt through day and night. Clear of the enemy that exterminated everything they knew and loved.

Silently we streak away. Stuck at the rear of the sled reeling Ulu in, I can't do much about our direction, but it doesn't really matter. There are red lights flashing at the edge of my HUD now. My air is critically low, but my body doesn't know that. My heart is racing, my arms and legs scream and shudder from exhaustion, but I can't stop. Not yet.

Eventually I get a hold of Ulu and they clamber forward, crawling inelegantly over me until they reach the controls. I feel us shift direction – for what reason I don't understand, until I see the corona around the edge of the nearby planet.

Then it hits me, we're heading for the signal array, the thing that first brought me to this system.

I nod. It doesn't matter, not really. My air won't last that long unless this sled is far faster than the shuttle I arrived in. From what I can tell, it isn't. Quite the opposite in fact. The minimum safe distance from the wreck will be hours away.

It doesn't matter, I tell myself as I look around at the yawning lightless void on all sides. The wreck is still vast in my field of vision, but slowly receding and I feel a sort of triumph in that. I didn't die there. Those things didn't get me. If nothing else, the unthinking brutality of what they did there failed. Ulu survived their assault. Ulu will, I have no doubt, outlast them all. It may not be quick or pretty, but they will be exterminated once the company appreciates what they're dealing with.

I turn to face Ulu and discover them inspecting the memory cube. Their hand looks damaged too, twisted in an awkward way and able only to fumble at the object. The harpoon's still buried inside and I can't even imagine the colossal damage I must have done.

They reach out with one free hand, a pale replacement one they must have salvaged in years gone by, to interface with my suit.

'Injury?' they say through the speakers of my suit.

For a moment I'm dumbfounded. 'I... me? No! no, I'm fine. It... I, I'm so sorry.'

'Sorry?'

'The cube – the damage.'

'Extensive damage,' Ulu confirmed. 'Limited damage to self.'

'I... good. That's good.'

The weariness starts to catch up with me. I'm dog-tired and struggling to think clearly. When I see something catch the light, behind Ulu, my brain thinks it's a star twinkling. Ulu moves without hesitation, however. They grab at me. I'm too confused to react before they've ripped the cutting tool from its slot on my leg. A moment's pause is all Ulu permits; some complex calculation going through their mind as the tool's jaws open. That sparks a moment of white-hot terror in my gut. Fear I've been duped, that this small breath of freedom is all I'll get. Then they twist away and throw it harder than any human could manage.

I see the light again behind them. It's a drone and my vision blurs with sudden terror. I don't see what use a thrown object could be. Then I realise the drone's accelerating hard. It doesn't matter which is going fast, the speed they meet at will be the same.

Normally a drone would be able to dodge oncoming objects, it's fifty metres away still but closing. I realise the on-board computer isn't directing this though. Instead it's the inexpert, brute-force mind of the virus and that has only one goal.

I don't see the point of impact, don't see what damage the cutter does. Just a flash of light as something explodes or spins away. I'm shunted sideways by our own acceleration, a new burst of speed now we're clear of the wreck. My boots press against the missile shapes at my feet and I focus on them, trying to get my brain back in gear. It means I don't see the drone make its return.

I feel our craft shift and the faint stars wheel. The manoeuvring jets spurt intermittently and at strange angles. Whatever Ulu is trying, it doesn't work properly but it proves enough. The drone sweeps up beside us, trying to correct but failing. It passes close enough to touch and in my dazed state I reach out a hand towards the familiar shape. It's long past though, but coming back around.

My limbs don't seem to want to move properly, but I hear myself apologising again – like a looped fragment or one of the wreck's ghosts. Ulu ignores me. I don't even know if they can hear me as they shift the sled and aim their weapon. It's short range though so they can't fire it until the last second. I turn, trying to see where the drone is, drunkenly raising my empty harpoon arm.

When it comes I don't see it. The dark shape against a black sky defeats me. All I see is the jolt of Ulu firing then a supernova before my eyes. Impact throws me back, so fast I don't even feel it. I can't see anything. Noises blare in my ears but I can't make any sense of them as I'm falling, bent backwards, something solid locked about my legs.

A shadow starts to loom, descending like sleep's embrace. I try to see through bleary eyes but everything is confused. My vision turns grey. My body jolts like I'm fighting off sleep. Random burst of light intrude, but I'm falling inexorably and then everything is calm, everything is black.

23

I wake to noise. Something inside me rejoices before I even know what's happening – just the sound of clattering, beeps and murmurs makes my heart sing. Then I realise there's light too, bright and beautiful and in every gorgeous direction at once. No looming shadows, no jolting terror. I rush towards it, eager to feel the sun on my skin, the embrace of my children.

I try to move, to sit up, but at first the effort defeats me. Slowly I open my eyes and the slightly grubby ceiling of the medical bay appears before me. A light panel causes me sharp pain and it's certainly not the open skies I'd been dreaming about, but it'll do under the circumstances.

When I do manage to shift myself a bit, I find I'm strapped down. My right arm is either gone or not responding, the rest of me little better. I try to look and see what's got hold of me but my head's also restrained and the effort is exhausting. Just as I start to panic once again, I hear a yelp and the welcome face of Sim hoves into view. She's grinning, red-eyed, sweat-plastered and every bit as lovely as I remember. Again, not quite what I was hoping for but events are coming back to me. I remember where I am and that produces another jolt – I'm alive, I'm on my ship. I'm going to see my family again.

'Thought we'd lost you there, hon,' Sim says, putting her hands on my shoulders to steady me. 'Wait a moment, lie still. It's okay. You're safe.'

'Uh... what happened?' I croak. Or try to. The actual sound isn't my finest effort at words.

'You're safe, just don't try to move much. You took a bad hit there, but seems like you're over the worst.'

'What?'

'One of our drones.' Her mouth twitched. I realise under other circumstances she'd have been grinning. 'There's some, ah, expensive news on that front. We're going to need some new ones. Most of them went mad and crunched themselves against our sub-space shields.'

'You found us?'

'Oh I saved the day all right,' she replies in a smug tone, only slightly forced. 'Swooped in and rescued you at the very last minute. Piloted the *Sak* on manual because some joker,' there she nods to the side, 'took our nav computer down and melted the comms for good measure. But I'm amazing, so something that trivial wasn't going to stop me. Don't think I'll ever let you forget how I saved you either. Jad did some fancy work with the shields too, but mostly it was all me being the hero.'

'Kall,' I say, unable to go further than that. From the pain that sweeps across Sim's face I realise she already knows or has guessed.

'Still in the shuttle bay. We've not been able to get close. Do... can you tell us what happened?'

'Drone. That cheap suit...'

I feel the tears start to come but Sim cups my face and

shakes her head as she stares down at me. 'Standard issue suit on most ships,' she says by way of contradiction. 'Only difference is you'd be dead too if you had a different hobby. Ulu told us what it was like in there. What was hunting you both.'

'Ulu?'

'I am here.'

I try to turn but the restraints don't allow it. Sim glances up, pointing at the straps holding me and clearly gets the nod because she starts to release them. There's a distant pain in my head, dialled down by something no doubt, but it's enough to tell me I took more than a bit of a blow.

I turn awkwardly, hampered by my right arm being encased in a surgical tube, and see Ulu standing to one side. Jad loiters nearby, looking protective – as though even Kall could have done more than inconvenience them.

I cough and try to smile. The guilt is still raw, but I've had longer than the others to get used to Kall's death at least. I'm half-numb in both body and spirit, but finally thinking straight.

'It's good to hear you – properly this time I mean.'

Their voice is different now, changed from the tinny reconstruction they clearly replicated through the inputs of my EVA suit. There's a deeper resonance to it, a complexity to the sound that's different to any level tone I've heard from a computer.

'Here is good. Strange. Unfamiliar. Difficult. Good.'

I nod and wince. Touching my fingers to where it hurts. I feel a cold, smooth surface there.

'Wha—?'

'You've had surgery,' Sim says quickly.

'Jad?'

The young woman shakes her head. 'Beyond my skills.

Subdural hematoma, frontal lobe trauma... You needed a specialist.'

'Then what's this?'

'Turns out Ulu is a quick study. Downloaded all our medical works then rummaged around in their toybox for something.'

Jad points to one of the missiles/storage containers from the sled. It's open on a side unit and I can see body parts inside. A forearm sticks slightly out, grey and metal, along with smaller plates and what I assume are internal components.

'You've used...' Normally I'd be aghast, but the effect of drugs and shock combine to just leave me faintly surprised. 'Bits of you?'

'Potential replacements. Neural components may be directed at microscopic level. Directed repairs allow prevention of debilitating damage.'

Sim grins weakly. 'We asked them to have a general tinker around in there too, give your personality the tune-up it so richly needs.'

'I...'

I hardly know what to say at this point. They've saved my life again. It feels strange – to touch, to think about, but brain mods aren't totally beyond the pale. Mostly they're done for medical reasons, both injury and elective corrections, but until it happens to you, who knows how you'll really feel about it?

Maybe it's fatigue, but the shock fades fast. There's a distant feeling of sickness at the back of my mind – implants and mods are one thing, but alien tech? I'm briefly horrified but then... then I don't know. I still feel like me. Still have the prickle of nagging worries and doubts at the back of my mind, still want to see my kids more than anything in the universe. And Ulu has given me that chance.

Whatever the side-effects of alien tech in my brain, I'm alive. That's got to be better than the alternative. For now at least, it's all just part of getting me back home and I feel better than I have any right to. If I start showing signs of change later on, I'll worry then. Ulu's shown me nothing to be worried about emulating yet. I can get over a creepy sensation if that's the worst it brings. Probably. Worth a try anyway.

'Thank you,' I say finally. 'For everything. This must be... You saved my life a few times and when you finally get off that ship you manage to rebuild part of my brain.'

'I am also rescued,' Ulu replies simply. 'Operation was not repayment of debt. If commercial exchange is appropriate in context, it is satisfactory to me.'

'Had you ever left your ship before?'

'Yes. Multiple occasions. Not unusual in the time before.'

'But that was all a while ago.'

'It is so.'

'How's the cube?'

Ulu dips their body and head in a sort of equanimous bow. 'Serious damage. Significant data irretrievably lost. Not all. Much remains. Civilisation not entirely extinguished by your action.'

'Uh, that's good then? And you? Injured?'

'Minor damage, higher functions fully restored.'

'That's just as well too, because our computer's pretty shafted,' Jad breaks in before I can respond. 'We're going to need an AI to sort us out – that or a replacement computer and maybe we're not hanging around for the company ships to get here?'

I ease myself more upright, taking my time and letting

her words tumble through my head. Even after they do it doesn't make a whole lot of sense.

'We aren't?' I ask. 'Why not? Isn't that my decision?'

'We've just been debating the point while you were out. There was always a chance it was my ship,' Sim says with a wink. 'But given you're mostly alive and still the captain, you get the final say, of course. Cos of our great deference towards you.'

'Hah – yeah, that.' I shift to try and Sim adjusts the bed to support me. 'Well, someone talk to me.'

'You've been out for a few hours now. Long enough for us to get chatting with Ulu.'

'And?'

Sim shrugs. 'Something you should see.'

Ulu gestures as they speak. 'Come.'

With a little assistance I get up and onto my feet, Sim supporting the surgical tube around my arm. That wasn't a threat to my life apparently. Clearly the bones had been stomped on hard enough to require some reconstruction work, but nothing out of the ordinary. The little medical bay is barely big enough for all of us and there's some shuffling around until I can be helped out to the main corridor. Sim steadies me as I follow the avatar along to the flight deck. It's a short walk, but I'm glad to get there and slump into my flight seat before I pay any attention to anything.

When I do, it all becomes clear. The wreck is a fair way off now, still moving around the night-side of the planet. Given the position of the sun, which I can see quite clearly, dimmed to look like it is a star in its last throes of life, it's still a while off returning to the light. But all the same there's a glowing edge to the wreck.

'The orbit is degrading,' I say at last. 'Why?'

'The game is ending,' Ulu replies. 'Opponent is removed from the board.'

'So the virus is taking your pieces, gobbling up your territory?'

'Operating below optimal levels. Consolidating position. Preparing resources for final play.'

'One that won't be ever needed,' I say with a nod. 'But the virus doesn't know that, so it's drawing all the power it can.'

Ulu makes a gesture with their lesser arms. I don't understand it and have to guess it signals agreement.

'Not alive. Not aware. Only function.'

'No sense of self-preservation,' Sim adds. 'Our computer's somewhat buggered so I can't tell how long, but the ship's angle has tilted. Without systems keeping its orbit steady, it won't be long.'

'It's going to fall, taking all its treasures with it. Can anything survive?'

'Records of planet lost,' Ulu replies. 'Salvage capabilities unknown.'

'But not easily, that atmosphere doesn't look a whole lot of fun. I guess any small fragment of tech will be useful to them, but it's not the windfall they'll want. Yeah, that's going to pose some questions when the company ships get here,' I say. 'Always a chance some captain or exec discovers a slight flexibility of morals when faced with reduced profits and a sentient AI from an unknown civilisation.'

'So... what do we do?'

I shake my head. 'Not a damn clue, but we'll work something out.'

'Ah well, as long as you've given it your full attention.'

'Hey, I almost died and I now have a half-alien brain. Give me a minute.'

I watch the wreck in silence for a while. If there's nothing left there, Ulu is a prize they'll want, illegal or not.

'No,' I say, thinking out loud. 'They wouldn't dare.'

'They wouldn't?' Sim asks in a sceptical tone.

'To kill us and steal valuable tech? Sure. They'd do that in a heartbeat, but either the company takes Ulu alive or they self-terminate.'

'No capture,' Ulu adds helpfully.

'No capture,' I agree. 'But if they did, they couldn't guarantee you'd not get out, physically or electronically. And if you do the AIs of Sien Nau would find out – one way or another. Enslaving one of their own after all that's gone on? It's history the AIs remember personally. The Filerich Conglomerate would be burned to the ground.'

'Proposal for action?'

'We tell them,' I say. 'As simple as that. We send a message, to the company and copied to the AIs of our home. We don't need a big announcement, that'll just make Ulu a sideshow. But we tell the right people as cover and let the details work themselves out.'

'Comms are fried,' Jad reminds me.

I shrug. 'Either Ulu can fix it or we dig out an emergency backup.'

Ulu repeats their agreement-gesture. 'Analysis of systems near completion. Repairs possible.'

'See, they've got it all worked out.' I let my hands settle on the ship's controls and regard the falling dragon ahead of us. It feels wrong that we're so far away, that it's just being left to fade from view.

'If the ship's going down, do you want to see it happen?'

Ulu regards me for a while.

'Witness to the final fall.'

'I'll take that as a yes. Sim, get us ready to jump into sub-space and run for home in case any company ships arrive beforehand. Best we have any conversation nearer to home. They're fixing to get their fancy engines back after all, we should make sure we're where we want to be first.' I hesitate. 'Ulu, I… I never asked you before. Your ship. What was it called?'

'Accurate translation is difficult. Significant cultural resonances.'

I smile. 'Give it a try for the simple biologicals.'

'Acknowledged. *The Light of Home within the Forest*.'

With a nod I engage the main engines one-handed. The *Sakakawea* begins to purr and surge forward through the great dark.

'Let's go and witness the last light of your home.'

ACKNOWLEDGMENTS

Every book is different and throws up its own surprises, but this one I never really expected to even write. I had the first spark of an idea years ago and set it aside because I wasn't an SF writer. Then the pandemic came along and I couldn't face starting a big new fantasy series as we locked down, so I searched my brain for a novella I might actually be able to complete in 2020. Even writing a short stand-alone while covid lurked in the shadows was felt like trying to squeeze blood out of a stone at times. The efforts of my family to keep me halfway sane cannot be appreciated enough. So thank you now and forever, Fiona, Ailsa and Euan – for all the support, silliness, love, laughter and hugs.

After the first draft is done, the job's far from finished, however. My brother Richard and Krista (better known as KV Johansen) both fielded early versions, random questions and far more general angst than most people should have to put up with. Thank you also to Dan Sutcliffe and Daniel Kelly for advice and beta-reading, Ian Drury for common sense and a final polish.

More thanks go to the quartet who helped get the book ready for publication – Jon Oliver for professional editing and at least highly-accomplished boozing, Mike Shackle for generously helping an idiot out with formatting, while Sarah Ann Langton produced such a beautiful cover she's probably the reason half of you are reading this. Lastly Angela Cleland for her excellent work and enthusiasm on the audiobook, may it sell like hotcakes.

Lastly, with SFF being what it is, there are a number of talented authors in these acknowledgements, so it feels wrong not to actually mention their books. Please do go check out the following, all of which I've read and loved:

KV Johansen – Blackdog
Daniel Kelly – The Fall of the Phoenix
Jon Oliver – The Language of Beasts
Mike Shackle – We Are The Dead

ALSO BY TOM LLOYD

The Twilight Reign

The Stormcaller

The Twilight Herald

The Grave Thief

The Ragged Man

The Dusk Watchman

The God Tattoo (collected tales)

The Empire of a Hundred Houses

Moon's Artifice

Old Man's Ghosts

The God Fragments

Stranger of Tempest

Princess of Blood

Knight of Stars

God of Night

Honour Under Moonlight (novella)

The Man with One Name (novella)

Fear the Reaper (novella)

Printed in Great Britain
by Amazon

78167185R00111